Wine Me, Dine Me, Dance Me, Romance Me

A Collection of Romance Poetry

Gene Hewett, PhD

About the Book

Wine Me, Dine Me, Dance Me, Romance Me, reads like an evolving collage of romantic experiences framed in poetic style. In many ways, the collection represents an autobiographical sketch in romance. It begins by providing snapshots of Gene Hewett's early relationships, evolves to romantic accounts as viewed through the eyes of a fictional son, and concludes with romantic descriptions provided by that son's daughter. The collection has a traditional table of contents, a second one, titled "Musical Inspiration" (which includes QR codes) and a third, titled "Photographic Images."

The second table of contents illustrates the author's desire to match specific songs, the majority of which are rhythm and blues, such as "Ain't No Way," to each poem. In the short run, the author envisions that the collection will be made available in electronic form, as a paperback, and for hardcover distribution. In addition, owing to the musical theme, the author anticipates that the collection can be presented in audiobook form. In the long run, the author anticipates that it may be possible to package the collection in a stage-production format (complete with a speaker, background music, and PowerPoint images—with optional dance choreography).

The third table of contents shows the author's ability to enhance the spirit and mood of each poem by linking them to a digital image obtained from the istockphoto.com or corbisimage.com websites. The majority of the digital images were based upon floral themes, such as "Close-Up View of a Pink Rose" and landscape themes such as "Wildflowers at Malibu Beach." Several digital image selections, such as "Glass of Wine with Cork and Rosebuds," departed from the floral and landscape patterns in order to further highlight a unique mood.

Acknowledgments

I recall hanging a favorite poster on one of my bedroom walls during the early seventies. The quote on the poster read, "We are all molded and remolded by those who love and have loved us, no love, no friendship, can ever cross the path of our destiny without leaving some mark upon it forever" (*Sun Ray*, The Thought Factory, 1973). At the time, I didn't realize the role these few words would play in capturing the theme that flows throughout *Wine Me, Dine Me, Dance Me, Romance Me.* Over time I have been blessed with more than one "once-in-a-lifetime," passionately romantic relationship. I have also had the privilege of experiencing several platonic, yet unforgettable, friendships. However, the true origins of my feelings about the beauty and grace and charm of women have their roots in my early upbringing.

I am particularly grateful to my late mother, Ms. Florence L. Hewett, my late sister Ms. Lynette I. Griffin, and my sister Ms. Elma Rowena Wilson-Vaughan. To each of them I wish to say thank you for instilling in me the confidence to know that it is possible to survive life's occasional heartaches. I thank them for helping me to realize that sometimes when I least expect it, a chance encounter may unveil the promise and potential for new romance.

In addition, sincere appreciation is extended to all the girls and women I've loved before, to all the girls and women who have shared their friendship with me, and to all the girls and women who simply shared with me a kind look, a kind word, a friendly smile, a passing hello, or an encouraging hug. Finally, I express a special thank-you to all the friends, coworkers, and students who listened to a poem, proofread the ever-growing collection, or assisted me in finding the right word or description for a particular line or stanza. For without the assistance of their eyes, ears, and suggestions, I might still be writing additional episodes to what could easily become an ongoing collage of life experiences framed in poetic style.

Contents

Musical Inspiration

"Introduction"
> "Goin' Out of My Head" by Little Anthony and the Imperials
> "I Do Love You" by Billy Stewart
> "What Are You Gonna Do When I Am Gone?" by
> Brenda Holloway
> "Hello Stranger" by Barbara Lewis
> "Hypnotized" by Linda Jones
> "Gee Whiz (Look at His Eyes)" by Carla Thomas
> "Yes, I'm Ready" by Barbara Mason

"First Love"
> "Endless Love" by Luther Vandross and Mariah Carey (1994),
> "Endless Love" by Diana Ross and Lionel Richie (2014)

"Reflections"
> "Reflections" by Diana Ross and the Supremes

"Somewhere in My Lifetime"
> "Somewhere in My Lifetime" by Phyllis Hyman

"This Masquerade"
>"This Masquerade" by George Benson

"For My Race Speaks the Spirit *(Por Mi Raza Habla El Espiritu)*"

>"*Cuando Vuelva a Tu Lado*" (What a Difference a Day Makes) Instrumental by Gato Barbieri
>"*Europa* (Earth's Cry Heaven's Smile)" by Gato Barbieri

"Ain't No Way"
>"Ain't No Way" by Aretha Franklin

"Ebony Lady"
>"Are You Going My Way?" by The Whispers
>"Mind Blowing" by The Whispers

"It's Gonna Take a Miracle"
>"It's Gonna Take a Miracle" by Denise Williams

"The Last Time I Saw Spring"
        "This Is All I Ask" by George Benson

"Stoned Out of My Mind"
        "Don't Let My Teardrops Bother You," by Dionne Warwick
        "(I'm) Just Being Myself," by Dionne Warwick
        "Come Back," by Dionne Warwick
        "Don't Burn the Bridge (That You Took Across)"
        by Dionne Warwick
        "Stoned Out of My Mind" by the Chi-Lites

"You Make Me Feel Brand New"
        "You Make Me Feel Brand New" by The Stylistics

"You're the Best Thing That Ever Happened to Me"
        "Best Thing That Ever Happened to Me"
        by Gladys Knight and the Pips

"Traces of Love"
>   "Traces" by Gloria Estefan
>   "Mac Arthur Park" by The Four Tops

"Firefly"
>   "Firefly" by The Temptations

"My Forbidden Lover"
>   "I Am So into You," by Peabo Bryson
>   "Feel the Fire" by Peabo Bryson

"Hold You"
>   "Hold Me" by Teddy Pendergrass and Whitney Houston

"Stardust"
>   "Stardust" by George Benson
>   "My Love Has Butterfly Wings" by John Klemmer

"Lead Me into Love"
>"Lead Me into Love" by Anita Baker

"The Power of Love"
>"The Power of Love" by Luther Vandross

"Vision of Love"
>"Vision of Love" by Mariah Carey

"The Greatest Love of All"
>"The Greatest Love of All" by Whitney Houston

"A House Is Not a Home"
>"A House Is Not a Home" by Luther Vandross

"Finder of Lost Loves"
>   "Finder of Lost Loves" by Dionne Warwick

"Here and Now"
>   "Here and Now" by Luther Vandross

"I Will Always Love You"
>   "I Will Always Love You" by Whitney Houston
>   "I Have Nothing" by Whitney Houston

"If I Could"
>   "If I Could" by Regina Belle (1993)
>   "If I Could" by Nancy Wilson (1988)

"Shy Guy"
>   "Shy Guy" by Diana King

"With Open Arms"
      "With Open Arms" by Rachelle Ferrell

"Going in Circles"
      "Going in Circles" by Luther Vandross (1994)
      "Going in Circles" by The Friends of Distinction (1969)

"If This World Were Mine"
      "If This World Were Mine" by Luther Vandross and
      Cheryl Lynn (1998)
      "If This World Were Mine" by Marvin Gaye and
      Tammi Terrell(1967)

"My Funny Valentine"
      "My Funny Valentine" by Chaka Kahn

"Whenever You Call"
      "Whenever You Call" by Mariah Carey

"When You Believe"
    "When You Believe" by Mariah Carey and Whitney Houston

"When You Talk about Love"
    "When You Talk about Love" by Patti LaBelle

"Nobody's Supposed to Be Here"
    "Nobody's Supposed to Be Here" by Deborah Cox

"Spend My Life with You"
    "Spend My Life with You" by Eric Benet and Tamia

"In the Mood"
    "Suddenly" by Phyllis Hyman and the Whispers (1984)
    "In the Mood" by The Whispers (1987)

Photographic Images

Figure 6 - Jack Hollingsworth, *New England Fall Color*, Photography, Corbis Images (ID: FSE068). This royalty-free image is not available at www.gettyimages.com/

Figure 7 - MacTavish, Sunset in Africa, Photography, iStock by Getty Images (ID 1128228758),

www.istockphoto.com/vector/savanna-landscape-vector-illustration-gm1128228758-297649682

Figure 8 - Robert Glusic, *Rhododendron Bush Under Tall Trees*, Photography, Corbis Images

(ID: CB014612), www.gettyimages.com/detail/photo/rhododendron-bush-under-tall-trees-royalty-free-image/654486470

Figure 9 - GomezDavid, *Springtime View of Yosemite Valley from the Gates of the Valley,* Photography, iStock by Getty Images (ID 537412380),

www.istockphoto.com/photo/gates-of-the-valley-yosemite-gm537412380-95284895

Figure 10 - AndreyCherkasov, *Retro Film Photo Camera with Yellow Roses*, Photography, iStock by Getty Images (ID 974185418),

www.istockphoto.com/photo/retro-film-photocamera-with-yellow-roses-gm974185418-265043397

Figure 11 – XavierMarchant, *Yellow Rose and Score Stock Photo*, Photography, iStock by Getty Images (ID 92022312),

www.istockphoto.com/photo/yellow-rose-and-score-gm92022312-4184125

Figure 12 – shulz, *Yellow Rose, Sheet Music and Wedding Rings*, Photography, iStock by Getty Images (ID 90164536),

www.istockphoto.com/photo/yellow-rose-sheet-music-and-wedding-rings-gm90164536-899080

Figure 13 - Bobbushphoto, *Sunburst under Mesa Arch, with the arches and landscape of Canyonlands National Park appearing under the arch*, Photography, iStock by Getty Images (ID 538143827),

www.istockphoto.com/photo/mesa-arch-dawn-sunburst-gm538143827-58547478

Figure 14 - olhainsight, *Close-Up of Red Rose*, Photography, iStock by Getty Images (ID 186324993).

www.istockphoto.com/photo/red-rose-gm186324993-27896046

Figure 15 - Siri Stafford, *Close-up of a rose bud*, Photography, Corbis Images (ID: 42-25747021),

www.gettyimages.com/detail/photo/close-up-of-rose-bud-royalty-free-image/sb10063721ak-001

Figure 16 - Robert Glusic, *Waterfalls in Stream*, Photography, Corbis Images (ID: CB001693), www.gettyimages.com/detail/photo/waterfalls-in-stream-royalty-free-image/599576778

Figure 17 - Danilo Calilung, *Glass of Wine with Cork and Rosebuds*, Photography, Corbis Images (ID: CSL2043). This royalty-free image is not available at www.gettyimages.com/

Figure 18 - Kevin Schafer, *Magenta Cattleya Orchids*, Photography, Corbis Images (ID: AF001661),

www.gettyimages.com/detail/photo/magenta-cattleya-orchids-royalty-free-image/527972194

Figure 19 - Grandriver, *Catamaran sailboat with a woman in the distance on deck looking at a red, white and blue spinnaker sail with wind blowing hard into it. The sea in a background is calm and it is a perfectly sunny day. A mountainous island is visible in the distance to the left of the image.* Photography, iStock by Getty Images (ID 466938932), www.istockphoto.com/photo/colorful-red-and-blue-spinnaker-sail-gm466938932-60684598

Figure 20 - Larry Mulvehill, *Lighthouse on a Rocky Coastline*, Photography, Corbis Images

(ID: CB014443). This royalty-free image is not available at www.gettyimages.com/

Figure 21 - Randy Faris, *Conch Shell on Beach*, Photography, Corbis Images (ID: CB066520), www.gettyimages.com/detail/photo/conch-shell-on-beach-royalty-free-image/654491560

Figure 22 - PictureNet, *Sailboats Moored in Newport Harbor*, Photography, Corbis Images (ID: SCA013),

www.gettyimages.com/detail/photo/sailboats-moored-in-newport-harbor-royalty-free-image/654494078

Figure 23 – jk78, *Long time exposure night landscape with full moon above the rocky Black sea coast,* Photography, iStock by Getty Images (ID 1308412457).

https://www.istockphoto.com/photo/on-the-moonlight-gm1308412457-398400441

Figure 24 - JAPACK/amanaimagesRF, Cattleya Orchid, Photography, Corbis Images

(ID: 42-26087773). This royalty-free image is not available at www.gettyimages.com/

Figure 25 - Carl and Ann Purcell, *Hibiscus Flower*, Photography, Corbis Images (ID: CB016047),

www.gettyimages.com/detail/photo/hibiscus-flower-royalty-free-image/529262314

Figure 26 - Kathy Collins, *Flower Bed in Park*, Photography, Corbis Images (ID: BRI070),

www.gettyimages.com/detail/photo/flower-bed-in-park-royalty-free-image/541209632

Figure 27 - Bob Jacobson, *Red Tulips and Yellow Pansies*, Corbis Images (ID: CB008959). This royalty-free image is not available at www.gettyimages.com/

Figure 28 - PictureNet, *Fallen Red Leaves in Grassy Field*, Photography, Corbis Images (ID: CB014221),

www.gettyimages.com/detail/photo/fallen-red-leaves-in-grassy-field-royalty-free-image/654492678

Figure 29 – nattya3714, *Akita Prefecture Summer Waterfall,* Photography, iStock by Getty Images (ID 1157247032),

https://www.istockphoto.com/photo/akita-prefecture-summer-waterfall-gm1157247032-315700759

Figure 30 - John Wang, *Trees on the Coast of Big Sur, California*, Photography, Corbis Images (ID: 42-25774668),

www.gettyimages.com/detail/photo/trees-on-the-coast-of-big-sur-california-royalty-free-image/AA011302

Figure 31 - Heide Benser, *Stargazer lily*, Photography, Corbis Images (ID: 42-19657368),

www.gettyimages.com/detail/photo/stargazer-lily-royalty-free-image/521180632

Figure 32 - Carl and Ann Purcell, *Schooner at Sunset*, Photography, Getty Images (ID: CB015654),

www.gettyimages.com/detail/photo/schooner-at-sunset-royalty-free-image/654504460

Figure 33 - july7th, *Columbia River Gorge National Scenic Area, Oregon*, Photography, iStock by Getty Images (ID 1164043688),

www.istockphoto.com/photo/punch-bowl-falls-on-eagle-creek-gm1164043688-319834420

Figure 34 - iShootPhotosLLC, *Monet Style Garden Still Life,* Photography, iStock by Getty Images (ID 173853902),

www.istockphoto.com/photo/garden-still-life-gm173853902-9506619

Figure 35 - Mario Krpan, *Trees and coniferous forests on the slopes of the Spitzli hill - Canton of Appenzell Ausserrhoden, Switzerland*, Photography, iStock by Getty Images (ID 1126372662),

www.istockphoto.com/photo/trees-and-coniferous-forests-on-the-slopes-of-the-spitzli-hill-gm1126372662-296507855#

Figure 36 - SondraP, *Rose Ring Stock Photo,* iStock by Getty Images (ID 89525203).

www.istockphoto.com/photo/rose-ring-gm89525203-2687126

Figure 37 - 167/Richard Nowitz/Ocean, *Cypress Tree Along the 17-Mile Drive Outside of Carmel in Monterey County*, Photography, Corbis Images (ID: 42-27337482),

www.gettyimages.com/detail/photo/scenic-view-of-sea-against-sky-royalty-free-image/1095497748

First Love

I thought I knew life, as I recall,
But when I met you, I realized,
That I didn't know life at all

Ours was a world of make-believe,
Ours was a world of fantasy,
I was young, and you my first love,
The world became our playground,
Crowned by a halo of blue skies above

The oceans, the forests, naïve bliss,
A constellation of heavenly stars,
A midnight slow dance, your soft dress,
Eternity's gift of a gentle caress

I remember your smile,
So full of warmth and affection,
Your smooth cream-colored complexion,
Your soulful brown eyes,
And gently curling dark-brown hair,
Your loving friendship,
So treasured, so rare

The fireside, and its flickering glow,
The candlelight and lover's row,
The fragrant aroma of soft perfume,
An awkward kiss, at the cabin door to your room,

I recall your gleeful laughter,
Splashing waves, windy fir-lined cliffs,
Your favorite dish,
Grassy slopes, and a lover's wish

That these few days would never end,
That I would somehow become
Something more than, "just a friend"

And I remember my heart's anguished fall,
When we had to part,
For reasons I can never recall,
Except that I was too young to understand,
Why first love, and endless love,
Might never, go hand in hand

REFLECTIONS

Reflections

Eyes the shade of foamy ocean-green,
Hazel as a smoke-covered ice-blue sky

Hair that reflects the chill of a wintry night,
Sparkling and glistening in a halo of moonlight

A light-complexioned Sista, with a welcoming smile,
Beckoning arms, knowing eyes, and teasing lips

A body soft and firm,
Womanly and tender

The smile and warmth and being,
Of one who loves, and is loved

Though we be separated by many miles,
Our hearts and minds, are joined as one

I live for you, and only you
My life is yours, you are my life

Wait for me my darling,
I will come soon

Remember me my darling,
Forever, and always

Somewhere in My Lifetime

Shimmering, glimmering, glowing,
Kaleidoscopic patterns of white, against a dark night,
Silhouettes of streetlamps, searching forever,
Illuminating, young lovers
Vowing to part, never, never,

Bright headlights, red tail signals,
Of cars moving much too slow,
A bitter throbbing in my heart?
Baby you'll never know,

That once upon a midsummer night's dream,
When your lips caressed mine serene,
Two hearts beat as one,
While love blossomed under a midnight sun,

I loved, you loved but weren't in love
As true couples who adore,
Still I secretly promised to be yours, forevermore,
You became my cause for living,
The very essence of my being

I am doing my own thing now sweetheart,
Only the fading shadows of your smile remain,
And warm memories of clinging arms,
Destined someday to part,

The budding wisdom of my broken heart,
Cries out in agony,
As the bus below makes its nightly sojourn,
Toward a scheduled destiny,

You were once the ticket to my every passionate desire,
My headlights and my taillights,
And I boarded a one-way Rapid Transit Flyer,
To a romantic rendezvous permeated
With jasmine-scented delights

But I lived in a dream world,
A sacred garden of evergreen ivy,
When youth and innocence,
Stood beside me,

No longer can I cast my pride away,
I count my blessings with each passing day, and
Somewhere in my lifetime, 'neath the twilight's
Dusky journey, somewhere serenaded by
A rhapsody in blue's celestial symphony,

I tenderly embraced a coed miss,
Who filled my world with meteoric streaks of happiness,
And shared the joyful bliss, of a passionate kiss,
Against this self-same skyline,
Shimmering, glimmering, glowing

THIS MASQUERADE

This Masquerade

Two worlds as different
As night and day,
Two polar refractions,
Diverging on their way

Two hearts caressing, two lips embracing,
Two lovers challenging, their inherited past,
Too naïve to realize, that it couldn't last

What brought the lovely Miss Ann,
To the Lion's Den of a Black man?
The pulsating stereo? soft blue lights?
Borrowed Mustang? or moonlit nights?

Or was it curiosity challenging sincerity?
Or maybe you were weighing in shame,
Sensual myths against validity,
But I never learned to play that game

Under a velvet cover of darkness,
You had a romantic interlude with Blackness,
The definition of interlude,
Depending on your consciousness

For one precious evening we shared,
The freedom and beauty
Of a world as we had never known,
Yet the distortions of reality,
Sought to force us into abandoning
This world, or risk compromising our own

I dug your personality, your pretty face,
Your soft auburn hair, and warm embrace,
Could we have been victims,
Of a masquerade in the guise of historical tragedy?

That today for Blackness and Whiteness,
There can be no sanctity?
That we are all puppets,
In society's production of irony?

That tenderness and caring,
Two hearts sharing,
Could never exist,
Beyond warm memories,
Of a lingering kiss

And when the curtains,
Separating Black and White
Divided that starlit night,

Two worlds stood exposed,
Before an audience without sight,
And acted out their roles,
As fugitives in hopeless plight

FOR MY RACE SPEAKS THE SPIRIT

(POR MI RAZA HABLA EL ESPIRITU)

For My Race Speaks the Spirit
(Por Mi Raza Habla El Espiritu)

From across the borders of Mexicali,
Over a vast Painted Desert,
Gorged ridges, a jagged valley

Past azure blue stretches of oceans churning,
Upon distant sandy shores,
Bleached and burning

From across the brownish-green waters of the
Rio Grande, came your culture, your tradition,
Your love, your land

And the third world encountered the Black man's fate,
Your sacred Virgin Mary wept tears,
Upon smoldering hate

Copper-toned Senorita, with eyes as quiet, and deep as
The midnight sky, jet-black hair, moist enticing lips,
The warmth and being of complete gentleness

Now your face is forever mirrored in my mind,
And the deep expanse of my longing,
Breaches all barrier of mankind

For your parents may have come,
From across the Rio Grande,
And my ancestors from fertile African land,

And at times you may speak,
In syllables that,
Only my heart can understand

But I know the meaning of your warm embrace,
And I Am held spellbound,
By the burning eyes of a proud race

And two lips caressed in passionate tenderness,
As two lovers embraced under a starry crown,
Two worlds met in Black and Brown

AIN'T NO WAY

Ain't No Way

With each passing day,
I know that there "just ain't no way,
For me to love you baby,
If you won't let me"

Will your love always glow,
Like the pot of gold at the end of the rainbow?
Or will it always remain,
Like an impossible dream,
A chest full of jewels,
On a bottomless ocean bound stream?

Though you're constantly on my mind,
And it's difficult to integrate
The collage of warm memories soft and kind,
And though the love I long to give,
Knows no barriers of distance and time

Though you are the girl,
That for the rest of my life,
I'd promise to have and to hold, and
Though your radiant personality,
Strengthens my desire, and makes me bold

Though your smile's heavenly touch,
Captivates my heart much too much,
And though my arms long to embrace you,
My life to surround you

Though the caution signs
Of collected experiences warn,
That I am moving much too fast,
And the rapid pace of my desire exhausts itself,
In a passion that could never last

Still, I know,
That for every little tear, there's a heartache,
For every dream of love, that longing can make,
For every gale of wind, that blows upon a rocky shore,
The message in my heart cries out,
You're all I worship and adore

And though I've walked this way,
And felt this way before,
I stand defenseless at the sound of your voice,
For I know that the tender bliss of your caress,
Is the key to my heart's sacred choice

A red-orange carpet of autumn leaves,
Dampened by a cold wintry freeze,
A barren tree waiting a springtime green,
Beckoning the singing robins, pink apple blossoms,
A warm summer's breeze,
While I await the only answer,
That can set my heart free

For I know, that with each passing day,
For every lover's quest,
For every moonlit night in May,
There "just ain't no way,
For me to love you baby,
If you won't let me."

EBONY LADY

Ebony Lady

Ebony lady, "Are You Going My Way?"
Bringing your world of joys, sorrows, and happiness,
Pull me close, gentle bliss,
Let your tears fall upon my chest,
Hold me long, moistly linger on,
Golden sunrise, coral sunset, never gone

Ebony lady, look at me,
Shapely, firm tender breasts,
"Mind-Blowing" smile, tease me dove,
Sweetly fresh, squeeze me hug,
Promise to love, honor, and cherish,
Parting breath, never perish

Ebony lady, "Don't Keep Me Waiting,"
Don't lie, don't cheat, don't deceive, believe,
That for you, I give my heart,
I share my life, I lay my strife
Forever surround me, in the afterglow
Of your completeness,
For you I hunger, I kiss, I caress

It's Gonna Take a Miracle

I remember the brightly printed scarf,
Gently caressing your Afro,
An inviting smile, a brown-eyed spell,
That held me so and seemed to know

I remember your smooth, honey-brown complexion,
Joyfully radiant laughter,
Softly sensitive expression,
And tender lips of affection

I remember Levi's,
Hugging you snug and tight,
My pullover sweatshirt,
That for you could only be right
I remember stealthy escapades—away,
Moist lingering kisses, warm embraces,
Lying close, breathing hard in soft places,
Concealed by nature-made hideaway places

I remember trying to forget,
That it was just a weekend thing,
A mutually agreed arrangement,
A climatic end to an autumn-winter fling

That to part was the way it had to be,
For in reality, your plans took you to,
Distantly traced places—an African Sun,
A career with room only for one

You wanted to be free,
To come and go,
To do what you wanted to do,
When you wanted to

Yes, "It's Gonna Take a Miracle," girl for me to forget you,
Because you gave a love, tender and true,
Now your face is forever mirrored in my mind,
And your love enshrined in my heart,
Through endless time

THE LAST TIME I SAW SPRING

The Last Time I Saw Spring

The last time I saw spring, I knew happiness,
I met towering trees, lime-green acres
Of budding leaves
Redwood-lined mountains, a gentle breeze,
Engulfing shallow brooks, and jagged cliffs

Raindrops fell glistening,
And as the world stilled, listening,
A nakedly damp earth
Rolled in moss-laden mounds

I knew glowing cinders,
Housed in scattered log taverns,
Connected by salt and pepper,
Bicycle-trail patterns

And cotton clouds rolled by,
Revealing an ice-blue sky,
A coral-veiled sunset falling,
A yellow-gold sunrise rising

So you see,
The last time I saw spring,
It was crowned by a halo of
Clear skies above,
Riding high on windblown clouds
Like a dove

It was running away,
In sparkling blue streams,
Evaporating, like misty distant dreams,
Chasing rainbow-laden hopes,
Hidden amid mountainous, rocky schemes

I'll never forget
The last time I saw spring,
The seasons changed, and I stayed behind,
To go to the places we used to find

To lie in cool shade, and toss smooth stones,
Into a stream that churned and foamed,
And tauntingly seemed to murmur,
"Gaze upon the face of your new love,
Her name is summer."

STONED OUT OF MY MIND

Stoned out of My Mind

I see your face mirrored a thousand times,
As I pass from day to day,
Along life's passageway,
Along a crowded, yet empty street,
Dodging misguided feet,
Sleeping alone, under an ice-cold sheet

I am disappointed because the shapely Sista,
In the halter top,
Who momentarily made my heart stop,
In the powder-blue Fred Astaire's
With sunlight reflecting gently,
From her dark-brown hair,
And who in the distance, looked so much like you,
False alarmed up close,
And failed to do, what only you know how to

She didn't have your radiant smile,
Softly glowing complexion,
Ebony-dark face, or warm embrace
She didn't smother me with tender lips of affection,
Tease me with an invitingly sensitive expression,
Or gently command my uncompromising direction

I am not everything I could ever wish to be,
But you made me feel comfortable just being me
Dionne Warwick would say I got caught
"Just Being Myself,"
With you I found an abundance of emotional wealth
Ronnie Dyson said you
"Loved, needed, and depended on me,"
And then had the courage to set me free

The Chi-Lites predicted you'd have me going,
"Stoned out of My Mind,"
I wanted to breach the barriers of reality and time,
To run the race between distance, time, and space,
Now only lingering memories are mirrored on my face,
As a lovestruck heart wanders aimlessly,
In a once-familiar place

Marvin Gaye said, "Let's Git It On!"
But the sincerity is missing now that you're gone,
Curtis Mayfield said, "Future Shock!"
And on my past, present, and future heart,
You placed a lock
The Spinners would say that you're "One of a Kind,"
Because you gave a love so rare, so pure, so hard to find

I awoke suddenly,
To a golden-yellow sunrise,
Only to realize, in my surprise,
That I could no longer reach out and touch your hand,
Distance, time, and space just wouldn't understand,
And my super-cool pride just couldn't hide,
The burning tears that overflowed inside

And my hands reached out in empty space,
Wanting only to caress your delicate face,
In my dreams my arms surround,
An image they futilely try to abound,
In my heart I miss, your moist lingering kiss,
And I'm deeply laden with memories of passionate bliss,
And of heavyweight discussions,
With a sophisticated Southern Miss

LA was a big Hustler-Player Convention,
In too many cases,
The emotionally expensive women's minds,
Seemed to be hung up in suspension,
On money, games, long shiny rides,
And plastic, showpiece dimensions,
On slick bodacious raps, and Afro-blown naps

They came from too many strange bags,
And glanced your way,
Only if you wore funky, elegant rags,
And too much emphasis was given,
To name-dropping places,
And celebrity faces

So I drove to Houston for a warm August vacation,
Foolishly thinking I was headed for another game place,
Hoping to run wild with my fast city trace,
Scorecards ready to discern,
The Sistas I could burn, but not earn,
Knowing nothing could possibly last,
Smiling in anticipation of a lightweight blast

But my smile faded when I met you,
My wrong-Brother scorekeeper quit,
And my heart just didn't know what to do,
I didn't bargain on your warm sweet lips,
Intoxicating perfume, and firm shapely hips,
Or on your flirtatious lashes,
Gentle kisses, and soft caresses

Barry White, "Found Someone," and
"Had So Much to Give,"
As we in our youth had so much to live,
He said he was, "Gonna Love Her Just a Little More,"
But I Forgot how to quantify love
Once I met you at the door,
In Time you had me doing and saying things,
I wasn't quite sure I wanted to
And soon my world, my dreams, my everything,
Became centered around you

Now I feel so painfully all alone, after hearing your
Soft soothing voice on the telephone, Gladys Knight
Knows I'll be taking that "Midnight Train" to Houston,
Dionne Warwick knows "I'll Come Back,"
And the shortest distance to you, will be my track
'Cause the Delphonics know,
"I Don't Want to Make You Wait,"
But with you happiness and joy have never been late

We silently pretended it would last for days, forever,
And inwardly dreaded the final moment we'd part,
Vowing never, never
In two weeks I must have advanced ten years
In stages of personality awareness,
All to become worthy
Of your wisdom and matured gentleness,
We must have gone a thousand places,
Laughed a million laughs in a billion spaces,
And joined sacred ribbons to our hearts
With forget-me-not laces

I remember midnight drives
Along Galveston's sandy stretches,
Imagining soft daylight sketches,
Of dream castles in the sky,
Among windblown clouds on high,
Exchanging passionate kisses in Herman Park,
Witnessed only by the dark,
Dancing closely to in-crowd sounds,
Swaying gently with the deep mellow beats,
Ordering mai tais and daiquiris, upon returning to our seats,
And holding hands in the dimly lit room,
Visibly proud of a budding love's bloom

At the Sports-Page Discotheque,
Hundreds of people were around,
But your deep brown eyes seemed to hold mine spellbound,
I had long since surrendered my ice-cold blue,
Every morning, noon, and night, my thoughts were of you

Your love, your warmth,
And sincere affection,
Were all I knew,
And I found myself whispering,
Secret words of love,
As if on cue,
From a manuscript written above

I trust the future to continue to bless,
And lead us safely through life's wilderness,
For even through bad weather there'll be tenderness,
For as long as it lasts, you are my present,
My future, my past

And even though miles apart,
An eternal place is held for you in my heart,
As together we'll forge our way,
Guided by a brilliantly glowing love,
From day to day

I await the day when our lips will again touch,
For I know distance, time, and space,
Will never hinder us much,
Your unselfish love must have been sent from above,
Because it proved to be a priceless find,
Blew away my game, enraptured my heart,
And drove me, "Stoned Out of My Mind!"

You Make Me Feel Brand New

Empty rooms, soundless laughter,
Gloomy hangover, like the morning after,
Half-restrained tears upon your plane's departure,
Memories of passionate love and burning rapture,
Of your tactically surrounding charm, and my heart's
Unconditional capture

I go to the places we used to be,
And pretend you are there snuggled close to me,
Ebony-dark complexion, slender, embraceable waist,
Full loving lips, gently glowing face,
Your favorite perfume's enticing trace

Packages wrapped with love for my heart to keep,
Surprise phone calls at night while I sleep,
Tender letters saying, "I miss you too,"
Your precious pictures on my walls,
Ever-resounding memories, like a symphony of waterfalls

I miss your presence and warmth and tenderness,
Your soothing laughter and breathtaking kiss,
Your kindness and sincere understanding,
The inner peace of mind assuring our,
Heart to heart's smooth landing

I was once insecure, unsure, adrift directionless,
Profoundly lost in loneliness,
You helped restore my pride, soothed the
Burning pain inside, and though I tried,
From your depth probing eyes I couldn't hide

You helped me find hope and strength
And faith in a brighter day,
We shared promises of a home and children,
And joys that would never fade away,
Considered navigating toward unchartered ports,
Or staying safely moored at bay

You helped rebuild my world anew,
Gave meaning to each glistening blade of dew,
Provided a windblown caress of completeness,
The sun's radiant embrace upon my face,
And the earth's bountiful harvest, from the seeds of
Courage, time, and place

You gave me a starlit night's sparkling delight,
Twinkling messages of love,
Flowing down in streams of moonlight,
Unbound seagulls in airborne flight,
And foaming white oceans of wisdom,
Beckoning me to come

You repainted my gray-clouded skies
Clear and blue,
Gave birth to a golden-yellow sunrise
And the fresh morning dew,
And conquered my world,
As no one else, could ever do

Only your return can make my every dream come true,
Bring back my wonder world of love,
And a heavenly chorus from above,
A chorus singing in tranquil harmony,
A song of timeless hew,
"God Bless You, You Make Me Feel, Brand New."

YOU'RE THE BEST THING THAT EVER HAPPENED TO ME

You're the Best Thing That Ever Happened to Me

Love was like the pot of gold at the end of a rainbow,
An unharnessed moonlit night's glittering glow,
Ever-distant mountainous peaks,
Abundant with snow

It was like the gentle autumn breeze,
Rustling through towering eucalyptus trees,
Fresh morning dew, glistening upon fallen leaves,
Slowly shifting shade, beneath a lakeside shanty's eves

And then you came into my life, my ebony-toned beauty,
Dark-brown eyes, sweetness and sincerity personified,
Straight brown hair, golden earrings hanging near,
Delicate lips, firm shapely hips, slender waist, soft embrace

And I immersed myself in your love's soothing stream,
And found the answer to a long-searched dream,
You held the key that set me free, brought warmth
To my winter-chilled world and loved me, for me

Like a spring-green sapling from Mother Nature's seed,
You became my joy, my strength,
The fulfillment of my every need,
As face-to-face my arms embraced, warmth and tenderness,
Beyond limits of passionate bliss

You're my heart's every desire,
The spark that rekindled my blazing fire,
And like ever-surging waves,
Pounding upon a sandy summer shore,
You provided a rhapsody of infinite love,
Each pitch resounding higher than before

I once stumbled through life, struggling in useless strife,
Trying to make be, what wasn't meant for me,
My heart once bore, the scars of half-healed mistakes,
My face the weariness of
Disappointment and unlucky breaks

It was as though I had vision, but couldn't see,
Beyond camouflaged spaces and perfumed traces,
Beyond mascara-lined eyes,
Beckoning to nowhere places, heartaches, and disgraces,
And I've known the backstabbing pain
Behind smiling faces

I was once alone, adrift on a merciless sea,
Your love provided a chain,
Each link leading me away from pain,
You rescued my heart, and set me free,
And in my life you'll always be,
The best thing that ever happened to me

TRACES OF LOVE

Traces of Love

Traces of love, will always linger on,
Long after you're gone,
Long after the photographs and souvenirs,
Have been neatly placed away,
Long after the patent answers to curious inquiries,
Lose their necessity from day to day

I'll remember your smooth ebony skin,
Dimpled cheeks, and long brown hair,
The silken yellow evening gown,
You used to wear,
Your dark-brown eyes,
So full of tenderness and trust,
Your slender, embraceable waist, and enticing bust

You're gone now, and I share the blame,
Forgive me if I caused you anguish or pain,
I fell in love with love,
And ignored the vital signs,
Sensuous pleasures, confidences shared together,
Now left far behind

I thought I knew you, thought I knew you well,
But distance and time often camouflage,
What only sharing day by day can tell,
We had a fly-in, fly-out, fantasy affair,
When you left only echoes of emptiness,
And heartbreaking memories lingered here

I foolishly ignored where each of us,
Was coming from, too busy I guess,
Making romantic vows in the sun,
We never seemed to have time to sort out,
How our hopes and dreams,
And plans for future things, could become one

Instead, I blindly sought,
To shoot the raging rapids of love,
Inner words of caution, held in vain,
And forced myself upon the jagged rocks,
Of reality, loneliness, and pain

There will be another, but none such as you,
There will be another,
To help make my every dream come true,
To share long strolls in shady-lane parks,
Tossing coins and wishes in bubbling white streams,
Exchanging passionate kisses in the dark

I wish you understanding and
Companionship on moonlit nights,
Promises of hope and peace and
Sun showers of brighter days,
Shooting stars of happiness to guide your gentle ways,
And when the chilling storms of winter, hover above,
I wish your paths, to be warmed with love

And after all the loves of my life,
After all the joys, tears, and strife,
I'll remember watching you walk away,
Long after the pain had fled my heart,
Long after the Miracle Worker,
Of hopes, and fantasies, had torn us apart

FIREFLY

Firefly

May love and beauty,
Always be your guide,
Radiant sweetness, and personality,
Your innermost pride,
Blossoming womanhood understood

Today an unlimited horizon,
The beckoning warmth of a glowing sun
Tomorrow flying high,
Navigating distant dreams,
By a starlit sky

Soon the runway will clear, flashing
Takeoff beams, will appear,
But I'll never say goodbye,
You've touched my heart,
"Firefly."

My Forbidden Lover

I once outstretched my arms to embrace,
A stream of glowing sunrays,
Tried to cradle their warmth to my body,
And became imprisoned in the morning haze,
Sunrays as elusive as your radiance, and charm,
Like your "Infini" perfumed trail which never lingers,
Slipping away as so many grains of sand through my fingers

I once pressed my lips against yours, tenderly,
Exploring every soft curvature, gingerly,
Hoping to permanently enrapture,
My teasingly resistant capture,
Foolishly seeking to control,
Tidal waves of emotion flowing from my soul,
Unharnessed desire generating,
Passionate crescendos of raging fire

I close my eyes and envision your slender, shapely body,
Your smooth copper-toned complexion,
Flirtatious hazel-green eyes of affection,
Your sandy-brown hair, gently caressing a delicate face,
Nefertiti's precious gift to the Black man's race,
Full lips, firm breasts, thighs and hips,
An embraceable narrow waist,
And soft, silk-like shoulders upon which hungry kisses taste

And yet, you are my forbidden lover,
And as long as I feel as I do, I know there can be no other,
Despite the lighthouse flare, and the warning buoys there,
I Navigate my heart toward this unpredictable affair,
Blindly yet boldly daring to dare

Your closeness has provided me,
A constellation of heavenly memories,
Upon which to chart my course,
Memories of soul-searching sharing,
In late-evening discourse
Memories of you combining your magnetism,
To a George Benson "Unchained Melody" serenade

To the gracefully choreographed movements,
Of the Los Angeles Ballet,
Memories of warm summer nights,
And musically colorful fantasia in Griffith Park,
You and I, in a crowd, and yet alone, in the dark,
Under a cosmos of ever-changing, and infinitely stretching
Midnight skies, that seemed to sparkle
With a thousand brilliant fireflies,

Memories of you responding
With the warmth of your laughter,
To the playwright-scripted humor of a Hollywood Actor,
Of you casting your alluring spell upon the soft lights,
And evening delights of a towering seashore diner,
Of a candlelit table for two at home, alone, and later,
Listening to a soulful rendition of "Ooh Baby, Baby,"
By Smokey Robinson and the Miracles,
While relaxing on a living room recliner.

Memories of us slow dancing to the sensual vocal styling,
Of Peabo Bryson singing, "I'm So into You,"
And of you pressing your body close to mine,
Gently encircling your arms divine,
Our heart-to-heart embrace,
Forever entwined

Perhaps the sanctuary of your love,
Was meant for another to share,
Perhaps I am asking much too much,
To always want you near,
Today your freedom is a priceless possession,
You are not willing to spare,
Outwardly I try to make no demands,
While inwardly you know that I care

I sail my heart toward a truce and alliance,
With a youth and wanderlust you have yet to explore,
While time sways in breathless suspense,
Awaiting the welcoming torches at your harbor's door,
Despite words of caution, I trust in you, I believe in you,
And have faith that the guidance from our closeness,
Will someday steer me true

Let me be the one you choose to engulf,
In your seemingly vast expanse of insatiable longing,
When your heart needs a friend, a lover, a brother,
When the world seems lonely and cold,
The feelings I try so futilely to hide,
Will never drift afar or grow old

There comes a time in everyone's life,
Of forking paths to choose,
Of faraway shores, unknown depths to explore,
Of rainbows arching, where distant seagulls soar,
A time of laughter and crying, of quiet reclining,
And reflective sighing

And in times of restless desire,
When the melodic lyrics of Peabo's "Feel the Fire,"
Are lapping at your shores, My forbidden lover,
For me there can be no other, and in your heart,
You know, I am yours

Hold You

I wasn't really sure, what to expect that day,
And then I felt a force, a tug, a beckoning call,
An eerie, yet gentle sway
I turned and met your brown-eyed gaze,
Trusting, sensitive, and warm
One glance, one breathtaking view, and I knew,
I was enraptured by the spirit of future romance

A mirage, a secretly veiled promise of unharnessed emotion,
Camouflaging fathomless depths of unchartered devotion,
Perchance? never again would I wander alone,
Through this world of random circumstance,
For I had been rendered spellbound,
Entwined by the silken ribbons of your impending advance
A mysteriously woven web, spun tenderly
By a lover's dance

A five-foot-seven, slender, sexy, frame,
An ebony-eyed princess destined to rival Nefertiti's fame,
Shoulder-length brown curly hair, embracing your face
In a wind-tasseled caress,
Accentuated by a white chiffon blouse,
And knee-length gray woolen dress
High cheekbones complimenting
A lightly bronzed complexion,
Full rich lips, and dark-brown eyes of affection

I had a thousand questions,
But couldn't find the words to express,
The pure and simple honesty I sensed,
As our eyes tenderly caressed,

In a quandary, I chose to ask nothing at all,
Choosing merely to let my instincts and your actions,
Steer me clear of an emotional fall,
And like a synchronized swimmer, gliding through
A watery ballet, cast aside all doubts and fears,
And let the rhythmic tides of passion, choreograph my way

In time, I came to understand, the rare essence of that day,
To know the cling of your arms about my neck,
The warmth of your body as we lay,
To learn the joy of exploring firm breasts, thighs, and hips,
Of tasting moist kisses of plum-pink, on gently parted lips,
Lulled by the soft murmur
Of the New York taint in your voice,
Your teasing ways, and half-hearted resistance,
Perhaps by design, perhaps by choice,
Positivity personified, and the heavens rejoiced

But like the ominous gray and black clouds, that hovered
Above, in time I also learned of impending danger,
Felt the threat of pain from a far-off stranger,
A silent torch you once carried,
That flickered but still burned,
A smoldering ember of emotion,
Rekindled by an undampened yearn,
I held you close, and listened to your confession,
Yet felt powerless anew, only time and caring,
Tenderness and sharing could undo,
The years of memories, held hostage inside you

And when the pervasive clouds of reality, finally engulf our
World, in a seemingly relentless downpour of wet and wind,
They'll bring a drenching message of future hope,
In anticipation of the morning sun, a dawn inspiring new
Passion, rendering old romance undone,
And may the tears of a thousand lovers past,
Flow down upon your face and breasts, may they moisten
Your sandy parched memories of yesterdays, and nurture
Tomorrow's fertile-green promise of completeness

May you envision a chorus of Angels,
Reciting this sacred vow,
"Build another life in his world,
Find another dream, as your fantasies unfurl,
Embrace another hope in his arms,
Feel the warmth of a mightier fire,
As you brave the glowing coals of his charms

"Share his world of love and laughter,
Navigating distant shores, beneath windblown sails,
In search of exotic adventure,
Under a constellation of dazzling planetary stars,
Arrayed like cosmic diamonds, on a black-velvet drop cloth,
And shimmering in the night in amorous rapture,
Fill his home with sunlight flowing, through thinly veiled
Curtain doors, casting intermittent, shadowy patterns,
Upon a glistening kitchen floor, silhouetting the study,
Where you'll pen beautiful imagery,
Upon the memories of modern folklore

"Walk beside him as you greet the changing of the season,
Among autumn leaves of
Pastel orange, red-brown, and gold,
Nature's kaleidoscopic gift to man's reason,
Slowly making your way,
Along a fir-lined mountainous trail,
Exploring a Lake Arrowhead Village Resort,
Patiently awaiting its wintry-white veil"

And tonight, beneath windblown and stormy skies,
Emitting a cascade of showers upon my frosty pane,
I will kneel in prayer, and gently whisper your name,
May I dream the dreams of a thousand kisses,
Of fiery passion, and tearful caresses,
Of blissful suspense in the midst of heavenly thunder,
Of unheralded rapture, casting caution asunder,

Of agony and ecstasy, hopelessly
Entangled in a turbulent fight,
Of a hero and heroine clinging desperately,
To the precipice of a heartache's plight,
"And I will hold you, and touch you,
And make you my woman, tonight."

Stardust

I tried to remember
When you weren't there,
It seems as though
I've always cared

From the day I reached for your number,
With a trembling hand,
Through changing seasons—I knew of another,
But chose to simply understand

I close my eyes and envision
Your smooth copper-toned skin,
The gentle press of your breasts next to me,
The dimple in your chin

The unforgettable soft, moist, feel
Of your gently parted lips,
The beckoning lure
Of shapely French Jean-framed hips

Your dark-brown hair, shoulder-length style,
Gingerly caressing a delicate profile,
And I bask in the glow,
Of your soulful brown eyes, and radiant smile

In defense, I tried pursuing women of fortune and FAME,
The ending to my infatuated rendezvous always the same,
Drawn again to your intoxicating perfume-scented trail,
Like a moth to a flame

Smothered in my dreams by an avalanche of
Coral melon lip-gloss kisses, as I murmured your name,
A series of interwoven memories,
Comprising the unbreakable links in your chain

Memories of you at the '84 Olympic Finals,
Looking World Class in French-cut Levi,
And later appearing even more elegant, at
An evening gown sequined—Black Tie

Of the tender touch of your hand in mine,
Your embraceable narrow waist, and unknowingly
Sexy recline, your independent, yet dependable command,
The seemingly boundless depths
Of your wisdom to understand

Memories of you doing the wave,
At Laker-Raider, Forum-Coliseum Arenas,
Of your sophisticated admiration of Firebird,
Performed by Dance Theater of Harlem Ballerinas,

Of candlelit sandwiches for two on a VCR tray,
And wine and roses birthday dinners in Marina del Rey,
Of you by my fireplace, on a stardust wintry night,
And of me, under the jasmine-scented spell of
Summer Greek-Amphitheater skies, softly whispering,
"Starlight, Star Bright."

LEAD ME INTO LOVE

Lead Me into Love

Spellbound, I gazed out my window for a garden view,
And there among a kaleidoscope of morning rays,
I saw a Mariah-like vision of you,
A crown made of white Lily of the Nile, and
Soft pink Queen Elizabeth rose petals, adorned your hair

I saw a five-foot-five, shapely,
Brown-eyed image of you,
Envisioned your smooth, silk-like, copper-toned
Complexion, felt the unknowingly inviting lure
Of your tease-me affection

Saw your gently curling sandy-brown hair,
Accentuating the lightly blushed rouge on your cheeks,
With wind-tasseled respect,
And gingerly woven in French braid, down the nape,
Of your sun-caressed neck

A bright red Tuxedo rose was behind your ear,
A trail peppered with pink Duet, white trimmed in
Lime-green JFK, and burgundy-red Mr. Lincoln rose petals
Beckoned me there,
To your star jasmine-scented throne - easy chair

A bouquet of Bewitched pink and white Honor roses
In your hand, a torch handle woven from
African violet stems and topped with,
Fiery-red Ole' and JFK roses at your left's command,
A gown of white, lined with pastel-pink azalea bells,
Rested on your nightstand

And, as if on cue, a chorus of hummingbirds,
Perched high in flowering white oleander trees,
Seemed to harmonize in the morning breeze,
As the heavens rejoiced above towering
Avocado-green leaves

Emitting softly, sweet lyrics,
As if sent from above,
Anita Baker's soulful rendition of,
"Lead Me into Love"

And now, as our new passions overflow,
My heartbeat desperately struggles for control,
If our love based on friendship, is destined to be so strong,
Then something truly magical is coming on

"Let your love light the way for me,
For without your touch I cannot see,"
Humbled, I fell to one knee
Before this miracle sent from above,
And breathlessly whispered,
"Honey take my heart, and lead me into love."

THE POWER OF LOVE

The Power of Love

Have you ever felt the force of a summer's gale,
Behind a towering red-white-and-blue catamaran sail,
As you glided through gently rolling, foaming blue seas,
Tasted briny spray on your lips, in the windblown breeze,
Felt the might of ever-surging waves against your bow and
Stern, crashing across your deck in random unconcern

Been rendered breathless,
By the beauty of freshly fallen autumn leaves,
Draped in red-orange, and tan-yellow mounds,
Around the base of,
Nakedly ascending brown maple trees

Felt the wet and weight,
Of a stormy winter's wrath,
Or the chilled rush of a brisk wind across your path,
As you struggled to maintain balance,
Through your thunder shower impeded advance

Been rendered spellbound,
By the magnificence of lime-green leaves,
Adorning budding pink apple blossoms,
Serenaded in the springtide breeze,
By bamboo chimes, hanging from
Neighboring townhouse eaves

Have you ever laid down to rest, under
A constellation of dazzling stars,
Been lulled to a dream-laden sleep,
By the peace of the evening's midnight,
Only to be awakened gently,
By flowing steams, of golden-yellow sunlight,

Or paused to admire, a brilliantly glowing, red fireball sun,
Setting over an ever churning, blue-green Pacific ocean,
Contrasted against, a coral-pink sky,
Speckled with soaring, white seagulls which fly,
In seemingly suspended motion

Have you ever tasted the sweetness,
Of a passionate kiss,
And felt flushed and warmed,
As though you had just consumed,
Vintage wine squeezed from grapes,
Left longer on the vine,
Or felt yourself whirling, seemingly twirling,
In time and tenderness,
Mysteriously captivated, by an overpowering bliss

Have you ever closed your eyes,
And envisioned her gentle face,
Become engulfed by the fragrance,
Of her intoxicating lures,
Or felt the soft, warm touch of her hand in yours,
Known the press of her breasts, against your chest,
Or the cling of her arms, about your neck

Have you ever felt the radiance, of her smile,
Seen the sparkle, in her dark-brown eyes,
Or known the splendor, of her sighs,
Wanted To share Nature's bountiful harvest,
From season to season,
To be by her side, under shimmering skies,
Enticing rapture, beyond reason

And, have you ever wanted to awaken to her kiss,
Between each golden sunrise,
And coral sunset's precious abyss,
To hold her tight,
And become lovingly entangled,
In the twilight's solace

Then you've been blessed, with awesome wonderment,
Known the myth and majesty,
Breathtaking emotions and spectacular pageantry,
That can only be sent from above,
And you've truly experienced the excitement,
And timeless enchantment, of
"The Power of Love."

Vision of Love

Have you ever been asked, "what character, personality, and
Physical traits in a woman, are you really looking for?"
Only to find yourself rendering a terse but polite response,
As you Cautiously headed toward the door

Diplomatically electing not to reveal,
The labyrinth of passages,
Leading to your most precious ideal,
As though it were a sapphire diamond held suspended
In place, by alternating patterns of black onyx and blue-gold,
Lapis lazuli in a glittering necklace

Have you ever paused at the summit,
Of a sandy windblown cliff, overlooking a surging blue sea,
And watched the turbulent waves merge and diverge,
Upon slick and jagged rocks, made velvet in texture,
By layers of brownish-green algae?

Gazed upward, in search of wisdom and understanding,
Toward the afternoon's,
Patchy-gray and powder blue azure?
And in response to your query, about this elusive allure,
Deciphered only that, she must be in love with you,
And you with her,

Perhaps she'll be like a favorite,
Well formed, and time-softened shoe,
You'll just feel more comfortable with her,
Than with someone new

In solitaire moments of déjà vu, have you ever,
Reflected back, on the road maps of your life,
Reassessed camouflaged hints and flashes,
Fragments and slashes, hoping that they would somehow,
Guide you to your future wife?

And like the distant lighthouse beacon, signaling
Safe mooring, in a fog-thickened landing,
Seen images of sweetness, a homemaker,
Kindness and understanding?

Images of one who is not overly demanding,
And who graciously shares,
Who has Nefertiti's touch, with lip gloss and fragrant
Perfume, and adorns garments, which show
How much she really cares?

She's irrepressibly sentimental,
Looks up to you, a sports enthusiast, yet tenderly gentle,
She's ever-charming, with a youthful flair,
And the sound of her voice, is like music to your ear

She's someone who draws her strength in Godliness, and is
Culturally aware, of your destiny in Blackness,
She's ardently independent, and yet, not overly defensive,
She shares your long-ranged goals, and objectives,
And is not overly sensitive

She's intelligent, practical,
And blessed with creative desires,
Is attractive, affectionate,
And can kindle your passionate fires
She looks good in a pair of Levi's,
And is outrageously stunning,
In sequined after-five

Alone, in the coral-pink sunset,
With high tide drawing near,
Have you ever peered down,
Upon the foaming white ocean,
Assailing and spraying your twilight dimmed,
And ruggedly towering fortress,
With seemingly wanton obsession

And whispered Mariah's message
To your woman-to-be,
"I have a vision of love,
And it was all that you've given to me,
I have a vision of love,
And it was all, that you turned out to be."

THE GREATEST LOVE OF ALL

The Greatest Love of All

The foaming white Pacific tumbled and roared,
Awakening a shrill cry, from scrambling flocks of
Hungry white seagulls, which lifted and soared,
Into coral-pink and wind-chilled skies,
As the golden-yellow Sol emerged from its murky depths,
To complete the morning's sunrise

Casting its mirror-image glow,
Across a choppy, blue-green canvas,
Of seemingly perpetual ebb and flow,
Creeping and spreading its warming reach,
Over a jaggedly rocky, and reddish-brown sandy beach

Embracing a brisk, and salty breeze,
Which scattered the dimming flames,
Of a fire that warmed you through the eve,
As you struggled to come to reason,
With what you truly believe,
Pondered through the moonlit, and starry night,
In search of wisdom, which can only be unveiled,
By a lover's hindsight

Reflecting back on the sweetness and innocence of first
Love, surely Nefertiti's descendent sent from above,
On the sometimes emotionally turbulent,
And anxiety-filled plight, of early interracial romance,
Recalling how you desperately tried,
To shelter your inner fires from extinction,
By the random, and misguided forces of outer chance

On your lifetime voyage of discovery, into the beauty,
And depth, and charm, of Black Womanhood,
Navigating their many spectrums of eye shades,
Shapely frames, skin tones, and spellbinding charades,
Reflecting on your forbidden romantic affair,
With a sultry and bewitching Sista, who
Seemed to only half-heartedly care

On a once-passionate and burning, cliff-hanging plight,
That left you tossing and turning, with seemingly endless,
Heartache through the night,
Or the surprise evolution of a friendship, that blossomed,
And flourished, through patience, time, and tenderness,
And to this date, has the power to hold you in check,
With a kiss, only an arm's length away from passionate bliss

Sometimes it seems as though you've,
Scanned the entire world from above,
In search of your ideal vision of love,
Occasionally clutching at a straw,
Hopelessly attempting to outdraw,
A Mariah Carey-like challenge to "Make It Happen!"
Then seeking a quick fix in someone new again

Someone who would help you feel
More complete, and secure,
Inevitably finding yourself wandering,
Aimlessly, from enticing lure to lure,
As though being in the right place, at the wrong time,
Was destiny's twilight zone punishment,
To be reaped upon mankind

Like the charcoal-gray and black stones,
Which encircle the now dying embers,
That once warmed you during your rendezvous with déjà vu,
It seems that with the passage
Of the glimmering starlit night,
You too, have come full cycle,
In the radiant haze of the morning's first light

Reaching for a nearby brown-and-white speckled,
Semi-dome-shaped, conch shell,
You explore its sharp, briny texture to reveal,
The cream and pink smoothness of its hollow inner core,
And recalling years of myth, and ancient folklore,
Lift it to your ear, to hear the majestic ocean's roar

However, what you detect, ever so faintly, ever so small,
Are timeless words of wisdom, from
"The Greatest Love of All," first sung
By George Benson and later made even more
Popular by Whitney Houston,
"And if by chance that special place,
That you've been dreaming of,
Leads you to a lonely space,
Find your strength in love."

A House Is Not a Home

As though overcome by a fast-moving summer storm,

The peaceful star glimmering early evening veil,

Became suddenly engulfed in a semi-permeable hail,

Of resonating booms of sound,

And radiating bursts of colors,

As accelerating mini-rockets arched and tapered

Into rainbow towers,

Which exploded and fell to the earth,

In incandescent showers,

Leaving grayish-white clouds to trail in the dusky sky,

Creating a scintillating fireworks salute

To the Fourth of July

And I closed my eyes

And pretended you were there with me,

Envisioned your joyfully inviting smile,

Tender lips of affection,

Your sparkling brown eyes,

And silky-smooth light-tan complexion,

Your gingerly curling dark-brown hair,

With crafted earrings hanging near,

The moist, glowing, purple-violet lipstick you used to wear,

The scent of aromatic perfume,

Intoxicating beyond compare,

Your unselfish offer of a friendship, so priceless, so rare

Spellbinding memories interwoven by the threads
At your command, of you in Levi's and pullover sweat top,
On the Cal State Dominguez campus, textbooks clutched,
Fleeting glances during a midterm week's rush,
Thinking of you while parked on the hilltop under the light,
A panoramic view of the sprawling campus,
Unfurling in the night,
Scattered with diamonds which glimmered,
And vanished from sight,
Of you and me enjoying a concert,
Or an intriguing movie plight,

Of you dressed in graduation after-five, and me without an
RSVP, at the bottom of a crowded, Redondo Beach
Cheesecake Factory's waiting list, stealing away into a
Dimly lit empty room, reserved for 150 guests, sharing
A tequila-yellow sunset, as the waning twilight danced,
Over rows of moored sailing vessels, and a yacht dubbed
Affianced, of you in the Crenshaw Christian Sanctuary
Choir, on the "Night of Jubilee," of me in the Faith Dome
Audience harmonizing with ten thousand voices, which
Seemed to ebb and flow, like a gentle sea which rejoices

Of me beneath the starburst finale to
The "Rockets' Red Glare,"
Thinking of you, with the moonlight glistening
Softly from your hair,
Of you thinking of me, living alone,
And of me thinking of you, whenever I hear,
"A House Is Not a Home,"

"A chair is not a chair,
Even when there's no one sitting there,
But a chair is not a house, and a house is not a home,
When there's no one there, to hold you tight,
And no one there, you can kiss good night."

FINDER OF LOST LOVES

Finder of Lost Loves

Radiating waves of moonbeams,
Flowed down to the earth creating a bridge,
To a steeped and rugged windblown ridge,
Rippling across its jaggedly towering height,
In diffused spectrums of incandescent light

Beckoning to an ever-surging and churning Pacific flow,
Which collided and ricocheted
Off dark and rocky formations below,
Catapulting sea drifts of foaming white spray,
Into turbulently swirling crescendos,
Which pounded against the sheer wall of the bay

And a translucent Blue Moon,
Seemed to focus a twinkling beam of light,
Upon this soliloquy rendered at midnight,
Orbiting the globe as a natural satellite,
Spreading its luminous glow,
Throughout a west to east rotation,
Permeating stellular skies,
With a sun-harnessed reflection

Searching and scanning,
From its heavenly perch above,
Zealously pursuing its destiny,
As nature's finder of lost love,
Signaling an exclusive invitation,
To this symposium by moonlight sensation

Persuading us to pause,
And gaze longingly from afar,
Enticing us to once again,
Wish romantically,
Upon a shimmering, glimmering star

Illuminating silhouettes of a first kiss,
An interracial Miss, an autumn-spring affair,
A vacation-sparked amour which was far from cavalier,
An Air Force firefly who took my heart to the sky,
Forbidden love, passionate bliss sent from above,
Friendship perchance? and campus romance

Calling upon us to again revel
In the seductive ambience of the moonlight,
To untie the hostage ribbons, which bind us to our plight,
Releasing them to soar into the rapture,
Of the windswept and starry night,

To experience a last-chance slow dance,
To sensuous vocal stylings, in the full moon's glow,
To understand that with the passage of time,
Knowledge and wisdom will surely grow,
And, like celestial music,
Flowing from an angelic choir above,
Inviting us to heed the timeless, and tender lyrics of
Dionne Warwick as she sang of lost love

"Finder of lost love,
It's never too late to find love,
Put the past behind you,
Keep your heart open,"

HERE AND NOW

Here and Now

The Saturday afternoon sun cast its warming glows,
Upon First AME Church's immense stained glass windows,
Illuminating their mosaic patterns,
Of colorfully detailed artistry,
Bringing substance and form,
To elegantly crafted figures, of historical personality

Highlighting in rainbow shades of pastel hues,
A spectacular collage of religious imagery,
Radiating in alternating light and dark spectrums,
Which seemed to leap, over the three
Parallel aisles, in crisscross patterns

Immersing the plush wall-to-wall,
Camel-beige carpet, in waves of flowing sunrays,
Ascending upward, toward a towering balcony,
Now engulfed in a quicksilver-like haze,
Cascading down upon empty rows of walnut-stained pews,
Which faced an elevated podium, and were arranged in
Jury style, to enhance the congregation's multiple views

I looked toward the alter in my solitary affair,
Seeking to follow the lead, of generations of parishioners,
Who once paused to kneel,
And lay their burdens down in prayer,
I glanced toward the choir loft, arranged in a
Semicircle formation, behind the pastor's stately chair

And marveled at the intricately portrayed mural,
On the oval-shaped wall,
Which depicted the historic passage,
Of the Black experience, from Africa,
To slavery's bondage, to modern day's freedom call

Mesmerized, I gazed toward the podium,
In this blessed house of prayer,
And centered among a kaleidoscope,
Of converging noontide glare
I saw a Mariah-like vision,
Of my future bride standing there

The delicate features of her beautiful countenance,
Slightly obscured, beneath a sheer nylon net veil,
Her low-cut gown of silken-white tulle,
Was accompanied by a twelve-foot,
Flowing white rayon trail

It was embroidered about her slender waist and firm bust,
With iridescent clusters, of studded white pearls,
Which blossomed in design like spring-budding leaves,
Her naked and smooth light-tan shoulders and chest,
Were gingerly embraced, by large puffy white sleeves,

Each sprinkled, with opalescent drops of pearl, and
Adorned with a single, alabaster-toned chiffon rose swirl,
She carried a bouquet of peach and yellow roses,
Embellished with, white orchids,
And green leather ferns, in her right hand,
With a gentle, yet teasing command

And, a chorus of FAME's Brookinaires, as if rehearsed,
Permeated the sanctuary, with tranquil yet melodic verse,
Emitting soulful lyrics, in ever-resounding symphony,
Which echoed, and reverberated, from the main hall,
And throughout the overhanging balcony

It was a harmoniously romantic interpretation,
Composed especially for this precious moment,
Of God's most sacred vow,
A distinctly timeless and tender rendition,
Of Luther Vandross' "Here and Now,"

"Here and now,
I promise to love faithfully,
You're all I need,
Here and now,
I vow to be one with thee,
Your love is all I need."

I Will Always Love You

Honeymoon with me in the land where,
Tropical sunsets set the sky on fire,
Where trade winds carry the sweet scent,
Of ginger, frangi pani, and passionate desire,
Where lush palms sway, in rhythmic illusion,
And majestic orchids bloom, in unbridled profusion

We will watch a master lei maker,
Create colorful garlands, fashioned in a flowery weave,
Go snorkeling in a world, embellished with iridescent
Sea creatures, and an intricate coral reef,
Exchange caresses, in vast fields
Of pineapple and sugar cane,
Join hands, while strolling through,
A macadamia nut farm's sweet refrain

Share a golden-yellow sunrise,
From atop a crater named Haleakala,
Romp in the black sand beach of Kamoamoa,
And later, traverse a rope bridge over a sparkling lagoon,
In quest of the coral-pink sunset,
Which seems to gently cradle our room

Spend our days relaxing,
Behind a thundering waterfall,
Enchanted by a lava rock oasis's beckoning call,
And witness a concert performed by
A mystical wind and wave band,
Surrounded by a sheltered amphitheater, of coral and sand

Vacation with me, in a world of endless splendor,
Breathtaking wildlife, timeless crafts, and historic culture,
We will tour the open plains of Tanzania's sweeping
Serengeti, to Mt. Kilimanjaro's towering majesty,
From the ancient island of Lamu in Kenya,
To the volcanic shores of Lake Turkana

We will sojourn through Africa's vast wilderness,
At first enamored, then held spellbound in scenic bliss,
Beneath an orange-gold tainted sunrise,
And pastel-pink sunsets that illuminate vast blue skies,
And immerse the rugged territory
In swirling patterns of kaleidoscopic dyes

In Tanzania, we will marvel at the sound,
Of an emerald-spotted wood dove,
Feel the warm evening breeze,
Rising above the plains, to embrace our love,
Experience prismatic heat, in successive waves,
Which engulf the landscape and bordering village enclaves

We will toast to our aspiring future,
Against the backdrop of,
A distant horizon's beckoning allure,
Observe a hang glider off Mount Kenya,
And a skin diver securing his rubber raft float,
Then tour through East Africa,
On the Catalina Flying Boat

On the Serengeti, we will experience anonymity,
On a more infinite plain, molded from volcanic ash,
Uniquely adapted to the grassy terrain,
And realize the freedom, of being on a great frozen ocean,
Which yields breathtaking views, richly endowed,
With showers of nature's love portion

Where every *kopje*, beckons an encore curtain call,
And provides panoramic vistas, of great herds of,
Wildebeest, and zebra in the fall,
Traveling in a massive dust storm,
Impaling a sense of hypnotic dizziness,
And mortal forlorn

You and I, alone together
Under a dazzling star-laden sky,
Testing the breadth and depth of our romance,
Against the supranatural power
Of the Serengeti's vast expanse,
Sharing exotic explorations in a domain where,
Sleep seems to be held in suspended animation,
While we listen to a continent,
Filled with ever stirring sensation

In Zimbabwe, we will greet the Hwange sunset,
Gingerly unfurling from on high,
And marvel at the land where, the lone acacia tree,
Defines the infinite sky,
We will navigate the Pungoe River, on a one-car ferry boat,
Poled by chanting villagers,
Through a crocodile-populated moat

We will traverse a plain, scattered with acacia trees,
Past giraffes nibbling thorns, and lofty leaves,
And herds of elephants, bathing in the warmth of the breeze,
We will journey through a land where,
Baboons lope alongside our taxi, in a hectic rush,
And warthogs dart helter-skelter,
Into the ever-thickening brush

Take pictures of wildebeests, a lone rhino, and buffalo,
And, while stalking a herd of impalas,
A female lion crouches low,
We will roam through hills, that are honeycombed with
Caves, some as large as the inner sanctuary to FAME,
With domed ceilings and floors,
Thickly caked with ash, from an ancient flame

We will be held in awe,
By the majesty of Victoria Falls,
As it plunges 350 feet,
Into the mile wide Zambezi below, and
Reaffirm our love in the misty glow,
Where Angels soar, somewhere over the arching rainbow,

As the river churns and foams,
Over the mouth of volcanic basalt,
It reaches the bottom, in a reverberating roar,
That seems to extol, in native lore,
Mosi-oa-tunya, or smoke that thunders,
Nature's symphonic overture in cascading wonders

Rendezvous with me to a realm of,
Sapphire-blue skies, balmy temperatures,
And emerald waters that are distinctly unique,
To the diversity of terrains
In Jamaica, Barbados, and Martinique,
From azure-blue seas, to a deserted beach,
From dense green rainforests, and vast arid deserts,
To an overlooking mountain retreat

We will watch scuba divers,
Off the Cayman Island rocks,
Sail in the easterly trade winds,
Which blow at a steady ten to fifteen knots,
Drop anchor, in a quiet, clear-water oasis,
Encircled by an unbroken beach, a coral reef,
And Crayola-colored fish,
Go shopping in duty-free St. Thomas,
And experience the excitement, and lure,
Of gambling in the Bahamas

Partake of sumptuous seafood,
In the resort towns of Aruba, and Curacao,
And enjoy the sounds of a culture,
Rooted in the rhythms of Reggae and Calypso
We will shop, tour, wine and dine, dance and romance,
And then, return to our private
World of intimate circumstance

Moored in a moonlit bay,
Under a dome of shimmering, glimmering stars,
Which seem to circumscribe the Milky Way,
I will gaze tenderly, into the Chaka Kahn heralded,
Eyes of my "Every Woman," with gratitude and love,
Eyes that rival the beauty, of the midnight skies above

And I'll promise her a lifetime,
Of joy, and happiness,
But, above all this, I'll explore with her,
Fathomless depths of uncharted tenderness,
As together, we'll celebrate our vows anew,
Serenaded by a tune first sung by Dolly Parton,
And later made even more popular by Whitney Houston
"I Will Always Love You."

If I Could

The herd of reddish-brown Arabians,
Tan-gold Palominos, Cocoa-and-white Pintos,
Black, and albino Stallions seemed to prance,
With pride in each stride
As captured in a choreographed stance,
The essence of the moment,
Accented by the unicorn's pointed lance

As radiating spectra of bright ceiling lights,
Reflected from mirrored panel walls,
The carousel gradually accelerated,
Into a revolving gyration,
Its circular platform whirling,
Against the earth's rotation

And a posse of wide-eyed, open-mouthed children,
First shouted, and then screamed, with gleeful laughter,
As their staggered mounts began
The ascent toward golden rafters,
Each horse moving in pace,
With the organ-chimed hip-hop rapture

The inviting aroma of buttered popcorn,
And salty roasted nuts,
The sweet scent of cotton candy,
And green grass, freshly cut,
Permeated the warmth of the expansive park's summer air,
As excited parents jockeyed for camcorder position,
In this ice cream, candy apple, and hot dog abundant affair

Alone, on a shaded redwood picnic bench,
Under pine tree-embraced gazebo tops,
I sipped cool liquid, from a frosty strawberry snow cone,
And watched you in blue Levi's, white T-shirt, and Reeboks

The snug waist harness, reinforced by five-year-old hands,
Holding tightly, to the Palomino's
Gingerly painted black reins,
The serious expression on your dark ebony countenance,
Revealing the depth, of your will to maintain

Tilted backward in your diamond-studded, bronzed saddle,
As if to defy, the rearing Mustang's efforts to un-straddle,
Ever persistent, in your quest to complete,
Destiny's imaginary sojourn, to victory or defeat

A journey which may someday, require you to negotiate,
The delicate balance, between career and future romance,
To traverse the warring borders separating,
Self-determinism, and random circumstance

To brave the blinding sandstorms of emotional chance,
Forebear against uncertainties,
Often veiled by a mirage's dance
And often obscuring from vision, crucial markers
Guiding you, toward true romance,
And away from wandering happenstance

And as I envisioned your future passage
Through place and time,
Precious lyrics from Regina Bell's
"If I Could," came to mind,
"If I could, I would teach you all the things I never learned,
And I'd help you cross the bridges that I burned,
Yes I would, if I could"

And someday when I should,
I will share vast treasures of wisdom's goods,
And tell you that a heart
First charmed by romance's perplexity,
Will never regain its original simplicity
That desired romance isn't just sent from above,
You must first have a vision of your future love

That you cannot direct the winds of offing romance,
But you can protect your heart from random perchance,
That in pursuit of new romance,
Do not fear life's unpredictable advance, instead,
Let the self-awareness gained, lift you to a higher plane

That it is difficult to enhance the brilliance of fiery passion,
And at the same time kindle,
The embers of a fading obsession,
That real romance soars like an eagle, in solo flight design,
You discover it one exhilarating experience at a time,

That if you accept the challenge of a blossoming romance,
You will at first be enraptured, and then joyfully captured,
By arms that embrace you tightly,
And intoxicating perfume, which engulfs you nightly

And that when you discover a sincere romance, you will
Realize, the enchanting powers of a warm, moist, kiss,
Which will first brush teasingly,
And then press tenderly, against your lips,
Leaving you hopelessly entwined in romantic bliss,

And generating breathtakingly dizzy,
Sensations of heat and desire,
That will swirl all around you,
Like a spectacular wildfire

Shy Guy

Kickin' it in the summer shade under a massive pine tree,
Laid back on the sloping grassy knoll,
Surrounding the half-court hoops near Doheny Library,
Sippin' an ice-cold bottle of Sunny D,
Pretending it was a Rocky Mountain brewski

Checkin' out the sprawling expanse,
Of the campus's Gothic-style architecture,
Accentuated by VKC's 176-foot towering clock structure,
Majestically ascending in red sandstone texture

Chillin' after an ol' school-boyz pick-up game,
Alone 'cause the not-all-that
Trojan wannabes couldn't hang,
Rather than experience the posterized agony of
Back-to-back defeat,
They faded toward the Olympic swim stadium,
In the sweltering afternoon's heat

Amused as I recalled lines from,
The locker room-inspired psych-out rap,
That I tauntingly chanted as part of my patented,
In your face, wazz uh Dog?
Shot block, whack attack

Word from the vine,
Is that my moves are so quick,
An' I lay it on so thick,
Most shooters blow their cool,
An' put up nuthin' but brick

I believe in the saying that,
The shortest distance between two points, is a straight line,
Especially if they measure a slammin' 38 D,
Are accompanied by a slender 23,
A 36 max, and she's super street fine

'Cause I'm the baddest OG at USC,
An' all the sweet mama jamas wanna be down with me,
Steady high sidin', an' rough neck ridin',
I bogart, an' I play hard,
I'm Michael J., Magic, an' Dr. J. all rolled into one,
I can sky over the Admiral, Shaq, an Olajuwon

I'm the love-machine mixer, the body stripper,
The undercover taker, an' the heartbreaker,
I believe in messin' around, an' gittin' down,
When I hit the scene, all the playa haters leave town

An' I've been known to sneak a creep,
With one thought, one goal,
One passionate burning desire to keep,
An' that's to pull the finest women in town,
In a Friday, Sad'dy, Sunday night sweep,
And then reclaim my crown, in a cold-blooded "threepeat"

So if your mind can't be righteously turned around,
For this funky 'nuff rap I'm putting down,
Then It's time for one of us,
To make like the breeze an' blow,
'Cause ain't no put-down strong enough to damage
My bad Ass, twenty-four seven, TCB reputation,
As double pumpin', reverse slam-dunkin', Joe!

Reflective as I recalled a recent letter from my ol' man,
Who says all God's children have a master plan,
Seems like he never missed a chance,
To drop crazy knowledge, and make hope seem like dope

According to him, I'll soon realize that true love,
Isn't about scoring, and it's a different kind of soaring,
And If true love really is the flava that I sava,
Then I should check out the CD by Diana King,
Who used to sing,
"I don't want no fly guy, I just want a shy guy,"

In his words, "Only time will reveal love's power to unveil,
A churning stream of flowing passions,
Which will cascade down creating,
A thundering waterfall of turbulent sensations

Generating seemingly endless showers, of crystal-blue
Persuasion, which first plunge to the very depths,
Of your innermost desire, and then radiate outward,
Like tidal waves of ravaging volcanic fire

You should always cherish,
Your visions of love,
For they are the offspring of your soul, and
The road maps to your preordained goal

There are two ways of showing,
True love's affection,
You can be the candle of its definition,
Or the mirror image of its reflection

You will soon realize, the rare essence
Of love's alluring nature,
And know that all it asks, and all it wants,
Is the freedom to explore,
A wonder world of uncharted adventure

And that the same power which can immerse you,
In a whirlpool of spiraling emotion,
Can also submerge you,
In a merciless undertow of forbidden devotion."

Finally he wrote,
"Screenwriters often dream of,
Romantic blessings from above,
However fate's ultimate toll, compels us as actors,
To reach out, and grasp the winging messenger dove,
To tenderly embrace our destiny,
And behold the miracle of love."

With Open Arms

Autumn embraced the sparse clusters of liquid ambers
Encircling UCLA's sprawling Westwood campus
With paint brush swirls of leafy orange-red colors
Speckled with intermittent twinges
Of golden-brown and tan-yellow
And framed by gently rolling hillsides of
Forest-green grass below

As a brisk and chilling gust
Scattered the assorted piles
Of nature's fallen harvest
Throughout the surrounding quadrangle's vast expanse
Into a topsy-turvy carpet of kaleidoscopic chance

The massive colonnades supporting Royce Hall's
Italian Romanesque-styled twin towers,
Merged to form three high-arching entrances,
Which unfurled in the afternoon's glow,
Like enormous Indian summer flowers,
Each entrance complemented by
Symmetrically proportioned balcony views
And accompanied by rhythmically spaced oval-shaped
Windows outlined in modulated red-brick textured hues

And as the diverging branches
Shed their pastel-colored leaves
They seemed to reach skyward toward an ice-blue sea
Laden with stratified white clouds
Adrift in the northerly breeze
Creating a breathtaking contrast
To the majestic auditorium's horizontal bands
Of alternately stripped, beige to sandy-red stone ballast

And everywhere I gazed I saw visions of you,
Your smooth caramel complexion,
Complemented by soul-searching
Light-green eyes of affection
The sandy-brown hair gingerly caressing your delicate face
The soft, reassuring cling of your warm embrace

Spellbound, I remembered the enticing appeal of
The sexy sway in your walk,
The New Orleans trace in your talk
Your outgoing, friendly style
The deep dimples adorning your radiant smile,
And recalled how your snugly fitting blue denims
Accentuated firm thighs, a slender waist,
And curvaceous hips,
Our first kiss, the warm, moist press of your tender lips

I saw you and me on a starlit cruise
Of oceanside harbor views in Marina del Rey,
Toasting my acceptance into law school at UCLA,
You with camera in hand at my May graduation from USC,
Recalled you, sitting next to me at the crosstown UCLA vs. USC
annual football game, and you surprising me with
Hard-to-get thirty-yard line seats
To this sold-out classic's fame

I remembered how you,
With seconds running out on a double-overtime plight,
Shouted and leaped with joy as the winning field goal
Barely hooked inside the left upright,
Momentarily oblivious to the throngs of disappointed
USC Fans, you screamed and cheered
And hugged me ever so tight, wisely opting to vacate,
We ended up sipping white Zinfandel by candlelight
In San Pedro's Ports O'Call, and celebrated far into the night

Later, after a six-month lover's-quarrel breakup,
I recalled how you first rejected, and finally accepted,
My heartfelt pleas for a make-up,
Admitting that I foolishly strayed in dating a breathtaking,
Yet inevitably heartbreaking coed miss,
Who lured me into her web with a tantalizing kiss,
And a "voulez-vous coucher avec moi," offer of untold bliss

As the early evening's twilight crept over Royce Hall
Like a dark, silken veil, a reverberating chime
Tolled from the campus tower bell,
Capturing the moment in time,
While releasing a message of bewitching charms,
One that was hauntingly reminiscent
Of Rachelle Ferrell's rendition of "With Open Arms"

"I heard that she hurt you ... she broke your heart,
They said that you just broke down and cried,
(I couldn't believe it boy), 'cause you were the lover, (Casanova),
God's gift to this world,"

Going in Circles

Reflective as I recalled a recent talk with my father about
You, seems like he's always had a way of presenting advice,
So that I felt I was hearing it true blue,
Advice like, everything you say and do in a relationship,
Is a reflection on the inner you

According to him, the key to happiness in a relationship,
Is the vision of love you bring to it,
And the key to success in keeping
Your emotions stirring anew,
Is making your vision of love come true

Adding that any successes achieved
In a relationship along the way,
Will evolve by mutual decision naturally,
My fate will be to embrace or
Release the vision to the winds of destiny

According to him, we may measure a career by what we get,
But a relationship based on the yardstick of giving,
Is one we will never regret,
And only some relationships are destined to flourish,
While most will prevail,
Because both parties are determined to nourish,

That to sustain a close relationship,
All you need to give,
Is enough space
So that both parties may live

According to him, a lasting relationship is a lifelong quest,
Not a sudden death victory,
To determine which team is the best,
And the primary ingredient for a successful relationship,
Is neither first-blush romance, nor passionate love,
But rather an enduring commitment sent from above

According to my father, the joy you bring to a relationship,
Is equal to the attitude you put into it,
Therefore if you focus on the brighter side of tomorrow,
You will never tread in the afterglow of its sorrow

Concluding he said, somewhere in the not-too-distant
Horizon, between a coral-pink sunset and a golden-yellow
Sunrise, lies my preordained vision, the charge will be to
Harness my unbridled desire,
And follow its signal-flair lead of beckoning fire,

I may not reach it, but the secret lies in
Plotting the coordinates to my heart,
In seeing, and believing in its stark beauty,
And avoiding the raging storms that could tear it apart

Recalling the lyrics to my father's favorite oldie but goodie
LP, that dated back to nineteen sixty-nine,
And how, in a mellow mood, he liked to spin it
On his turntable from time to time
A classic tune titled, "Going in Circles,"
More recently known by the Luther Vandross rendition,
And originally sung by Harry Elston of
"The Friends of Distinction,"

"I'm an ever-rolling wheel, without a destination real,
And I'm an ever-spinnin' top, whirling around till I drop,
Oh, but what am I to do, my mind is in a whirlpool,
Give me a little hope, one small thing to cling to,"

IF THIS WORLD WERE MINE

If This World Were Mine

Honeymoon with me in California's Monterey Peninsula,
And experience a world that is both enchanted and timeless,
Celebrate with me in,
Silver Anniversary's wedding-bell bliss,
Let's make a toast to twenty-five years of joy and tenderness
Together we will sojourn through a land of natural artistry,
Renowned for its rugged coastline, spectacular beauty,
And breathtaking combinations of land and sea

Where tall pines, majestic oaks, and wind-swept cypress,
Seem to cling passionately to the jagged rocky coast, and
Encircle lush green acres of rolling hills in a lover's caress,
Where fish and shellfish thrive
In the deep blue Pacific waters,
And share a harbor home with seals,
Migrating whales, and sea otters,
Where the five thousand-acre Del Monte forest terrain,
Gives the populations of
Native birds and deer a natural refrain

A tranquil realm steeped in early West Coast history, with
Father Junipero Serra, and the Carmel Mission, the Hearst
Castle, Crosby Pro-Am Golf Tournament and Steinbeck's
Cannery, departing from Monterey's Fishermen's Wharf, we
Will explore, the famous seventeen-mile drive along the
Pacific Grove shore, see clusters of well-manicured
Victorians abundant with lore, as red and pink ice plants
Reach seaward to the horizon's door

We will stop to admire a coral-pink Pacific Coast sunset,
Against the Lone Cypress Tree's romantically twisted
Silhouette, then continue on through Pebble Beach for a
Relaxing spree, we will view the artists' galleries in quaint
Carmel-by-the-Sea, leaving Carmel's white sandy beaches
And skyward-branching acacia trees, we will stop along
Highway 1 and listen to the howling of, sea wolves
Permeating Point Lobos in the eerie guise of the breeze

Continuing on to the Lighthouse at Big Sur, and the
Bixby Bridge, we will pause to comb the sprawling expanse
Of the Majestic Hearst Castle, perched high above the
Pacific on a Hilltop ridge, then on to San Simeon under
A glittering evening's veiled mystic,
Awakening to the sound of an ebb and flow tide's rhapsody,
Where the earth has joined in holy wedlock with the sea, and
The universe reigns supreme in blissful harmony

Although much has changed between us over the years,
Much has weathered the occasional showers of tears and
Fears, we still have our health and strength and happiness,
And a priceless son, who now shares his own commitment
To bliss, wedding his USC sweetheart last summer in a
New Orleans parish, I still admire the soft reflection of the
Moonlight on your hair, I am still intoxicated by the
Fragrance of your aromatic perfume, and entranced by the
Sparkle of diamond earrings hanging near

I still watch you brush your sandy-brown hair in the eve,
Notice the gentle sway of your floral-printed sun dresses in
The breeze, like to rub fragrant oil along the smooth
Curvature of your back, I still long for the sound of your
Voice when you're away, thrill to your touch, and chill to
Your embrace during a slow-drag track,

I am captivated by the seemingly boundless depths of your
Wisdom, and I am hopelessly devoted to your wit, your sexy
Charm, your five-foot-six slender presence,
And silky-smooth light-tan complexion

Reflecting on the assortment of high maintenance
"Waiting To Exhale," dates before you, the treasure chest of
Evening delights, the handful of, "if I coulda, woulda,
shoulda" forgettable nights, experienced along the way,
God's gifts of sharing, giving, and loving, received each
Passing day, I know that as the eve of our wedding
Anniversary comes due, as dusk falls over a candlelit table
For two, I humbly kneel, and place this band of silver and
Gold about your finger anew, here and now, in Monterey's
Ruggedly awe-inspiring splendor, the precious lyrics of
Luther Vandross's "If This World Were Mine,"
Ring ever so true, ever so tender

"If this world were mine, I would place at your feet,
All that I own, you've been so good to me, if this world
Were mine, I'd give you the flowers, the birds and the bees,
And with your love beside me, that would be all I need,"

My Funny Valentine

Argyle and Sunset in Hollywood, famous coordinates for the
Palladium's four hundred-capacity ballroom's regal flair,
Traditional host to dance, rock concerts, and today's
"The Power of Color," Ebony Fashion Fair

Honored that you volunteered to forego FAME's Easter
Egg hunt, and join me this sunny springtime afternoon,
Upon learning that your mother was informed, that
Her patient was about to deliver,
In the King Hospital OB Room

You seated next to me at a table for ten, each day looking
More and more like your attractive maternal kin, with your
Smooth caramel complexion, light-green eyes of affection,
Your sandy-brown hair, gingerly curling about a delicate
Face, the deep dimples adorning your radiant smile,
Your warm embrace

Amused as I recalled how easily I am swayed,
By your sad-faced pouts when your expectations are
Delayed, when you stretch on tipsy toes, to give me a
Welcome-home kiss, and by the feisty spirit
Of a sometimes-sophisticated young miss

Act I, Scene 1, and as the glare of the ceiling lights declined,
I could tell you were eager to let your vivid imagination
Unwind, probably envisioning your maiden voyage stroll
Down the runway, as the commentator's exciting,
Fast-moving intro got underway

Act II, she leveled off to a smooth, rapidly colorful
Narration, and you imagined the spotlights focusing on your
Every motion, as you whirled across the stage, to the
Heightened tempo of the music director's
Scintillating jazz piano rhythm

And you probably heard, "now dressed in a pink brocade
And taffeta dress, featuring a lace-on-crinoline zippered
Back, that tapers to a petite basque waist, with a satin-lined
Track, from Rancho Palos Verdes, California, is Shanna,
Wearing the perfect attire for a 'Put On Your Easter
Bonnet,' afternoon, that is certain to make even
The freshest young man swoon,
From Lancôme, France ... isn't she adorable!"

Seeing the excitement in your eyes brings back so many
Memories, of you and me at the Griffith Park Observatory,
Binoculars focused on what appeared to be a fuzzy snowball
Image, that seemed to rest at the base of the Big Dipper's
Carriage, as the comet Hale-Bopp and the starry skies,
United in marriage

Of you and me at your January, seventh-year birthday party,
Toasting the occasion with
Your Pocahontas crew at Mickey D's,
And you on a windswept and rainy winter evening, proudly
Completing, your fruits-of-life color-by-number oil painting

Showing a platter of red delicious apples,
For peace from the Almighty above,
Sweet, heart-shaped strawberries, for everlasting love, and
Scrumptious round cherries for joy placed center stage, with
Juicy purple grapes for good cheer and tossed green sage

And years from now, after you've had ample time to grow
Up, to follow the rites of passage, and drink from the plenty
Cup, your mother and I will share with you our collective
Wisdom, which began with first-blush romance,
Progressed to going-steady love,
And culminated in holy matrimony's kingdom

And someday I am sure, you'll probably concur, there's
More to life than make-believe, or an occasional fox fur, it's
More than sleek gowns, that seem to fit every slender curve,
And flow gracefully from the waist of statuesque models or
Swerve, like rippling waters over smooth
Pearlescent pebbles, disheveled

Act II concludes with a scene titled, "The Bride and
Groom," as the commentator/soloist's soft voice slowly
Permeates the room, building to an exciting climax, she
Sings your favorite tune, delivered in classic Chaka Kahn
Tear-it-up style, leaving the audience breathless,
And applauding for quite a while,

"My funny valentine,
Sweet comic valentine, you make me smile with my heart,
Your looks are laughable, unphotographable,
Yet you're my favorite work of art."

Whenever You Call

It was the second Saturday in December, and twilight wove
Its dusky spiral, along Admiralty Way and Mindanao,
Traditional coordinates for Marina del Rey's eight-acre
Burton Chase Park, an oak- and pine tree-laden grassy
Expanse, framed by the soft white glow
Of lamp lights in the dark

Nestled snugly adjacent to the Santa Monica Yacht Club, a
Little down the road from Moose's Restaurant and Pub,
Bordered on the north by sloops, ketches, and speedboats,
The preferred mode of transport being power cruisers,
A Pacific Coast winter wonderland in nautical floats

Picnic shelters, redwood benches and tables,
Were scantily arranged atop grassy knolls,
Which curved downward to the edge of the
Two mile-wide channel, in leisurely sloping rolls

And throngs of excited on lookers eagerly awaited the start,
Of the thirty-fifth annual "Christmas Parade of Lights"
Affair, seemingly oblivious to the frosty chill in the leeward
Air, as a brisk wind prompted the murky waters to heave
And sway, and topped the surging ocean
With caps of foamy white spray

Honored to be in the company of my father,
A former Navy Seal Explorer,
Who over the years made sure,
I was thoroughly steeped in ship to shore maritime lore

And suddenly, the star-glimmering sky,
Became immersed in a semi-permeable hail,
Of resonating bursts of cannon fire accompanied by,
Sparkling brushlike streaks of colorful pastel

As accelerating Roman candles,
Transformed into kaleidoscopic towers,
Which exploded and cascaded to the earth,
In spiraling showers

Smiling as I recalled how throughout the day,
My father's turntable
Spun his favorite 45-RPMS,
In honor of the holiday

Remembering how he paused occasionally to break into,
A chorus of selected lyrics, to Luther Vandross's
"Have Yourself a Merry Little Christmas," his favorites
Being Nancy Wilson's "What Are You Doing New Year's
Eve," and Nat King Cole's, "The Christmas Song,"
Tunes he more than generously played all day long

As the fifty-boat procession of sleek hulled yachts,
Catamarans, yawls, and whalers streamed by, some with
Flowing white banners, which read, "Joy to the World,"
And "Silent Night," rippling against the evening sky,
My thoughts inevitably drifted to déjà vu with you

You and me last summer in a rowboat at FAME's
Singles' picnic in Newport Beach, you attired
In after five—hobo chic, with hands tied behind your back,
Bobbing for apples at the
Sadie Hawkins Club Halloween Retreat

You and me during Thanksgiving break, watching
Whitney and Brandy in "Cinderella" on DVD, and you
Leaving a surprise gift under the family tree,
The note on the card reading, "'Cause our favorite song by
Pattie Labelle 'tis, "Somebody Loves You Baby"
(You Know Who It Is)

And as a two-masted fore and aft cutter goes gliding by,
With each tinsel-wrapped yard and boom adorned with
Twinkling lights, which signaled,
"O Holy Night" in the evening sky,
I think the secrets to my innermost feelings probably lie, in
Heartfelt lyrics to a ballad from Mariah's CD "Butterfly,"

"I won't ever be too far away to feel you,
And I won't hesitate at all, whenever you call,
And I'll always remember,
The part of you so tender,"

When You Believe

I close my eyes and envision your smooth caramel
Complexion, your infectious smile, and "shake-what-your-
Mama-gave, party-over-here style," your six-foot muscular
Frame, and glued to the tube focus during a
Lakers Staples Center playoff game

I recall the mischievous twinkle in your dark-brown eyes,
The aromatic scent of Cool Water when you arrive at my
Door, the warm, secure feel of my hand in yours,
The enticing curvature of your parted lips, and the "tight"
Cling of Levi's about your hips

I once confided in my mother, how much I really cared,
And she shared some time-tested rules, guaranteed to put
A little cinnamon an' spice,
Into this senior high affair

According to her, I should never initiate a call, and only
Sparingly return yours,
Included in this list of do's and don'ts,
Are pages, faxes, voice, and e-mails

According to her, I should be first to end all calls,
Generally restricting them to ten minutes or less,
And never accept a Saturday-night date after Wednesday,
As this could be a sign that you were getting careless

According to her, I should consider a parting of the way,
If you don't buy me a romantic,
Although not necessarily expensive,
Gift for Valentine's or my birthday,

And by all means, according to her,
I should favor quality over quantity, in my dating choice,
I should be confident enough to direct my own way,
And not drop my every plan at the sound of your voice

In a recent heart-to-heart with my father I recall,
Receiving, ol' school words of wisdom,
Which he said captured it all

According to him, when I decide to truly accept the
Challenge of a blossoming romance, I will at first be
Enraptured, and then someday joyfully captured, by arms
That will embrace me tightly, and intoxicating aftershave,
Which will engulf me nightly

According to him, when I finally discover a sincere
Romance, I will realize the enchanting powers of a warm,
Moist kiss, which will first brush teasingly,
And then press tenderly against my lips,

Leaving me hopelessly entwined in romantic bliss,
And generating breathtakingly dizzy sensations
Of heat and desire, that will swirl all around me
Like a spectacular wildfire

Well, perhaps someday I'll have a better appreciation,
For my mother's time-tested secret rules,
And my father's words of wisdom from the ol' school

Yet somehow I know what I truly believe, is that
The spiritual roots of what I am destined to achieve, are
Centered in the abundant grace and mercy
I am willing to receive,

And in the knowledge that in time,
I may experience joy in the midst of sorrow's forlorn,
And peace in the wake of a wintry storm,

And even though the future may at times appear obscure,
There's comfort in knowing that the healing power of love,
Will help me survive heartache's beckoning lure

For I know that the interwoven fibers of tenderness and
Caring, have the strength to form, a seaworthy vessel of
Papyrus sedge, quite similar to the basket that transported,
The baby Moses down the surging Nile,
"Prince of Egypt" style

In a saga about the first messenger to the Messiah,
A theme best expressed in lyrics sung by
The sensational Grammy Award-winning divas—
Whitney and Mariah

"There can be miracles, when you believe,
Though hope is frail, it's hard to kill,
Who knows what miracles, you can achieve,
When you believe, somehow you will,"

When You Talk about Love

April at the J. Paul Getty Museum in Brentwood, California,
Strolling through springtime gardens of earthly delights,
Landscaped to complement and supplement the,
"Temple in the Sky's" careful spacing of forms
And delicate weaving of light

Traversing outdoor terraces with breathtaking city views,
Rivaled by architecture with sweeping vistas of old and new,
To the east the rustic San Gabriel Mountains, to the
Southeast the sprawling UCLA campus, on the southwest
The Pacific ebbs and flows like an endless array of fountains

Marveling at the Central Garden's hand-sculptured artistry,
Designed to change with the seasons, a crowning tribute to
Nineteen acres of foliage and terrace majesty, surrounded by
An eight thousand-plus California oak-tree dynasty

Recalling that as the ascending tram reached the hilltop
Arrival phase, center stage seemed to be commanded by
Four Italian stone pines, signaling the apex to
A winding ribbon of skyward branching designs,

Which stretched along Getty Center Drive,
And pointed the way to a stately sycamore tree-lined
Entrance, that unfurled into a courtyard,
Encircled by an imposing line of Mexican cypress

Remembering upper-level South Terrace views, bordered
Along the base with pastel bird of paradise hues,
Admiring the South Promontory's cactus garden,
Where succulents, prickly pears and agave,
Accentuate their Southern California desert ancestry

This was once our special between-class rendezvous,
And everywhere I gazed brought memories of *deja vu,*
I close my eyes and envision your smooth caramel
Complexion, and dark-brown eyes of affection

Warmed by the radiance of the pavilion's natural light,
I recall the infectious way you smiled,
And your tendency to strike a pose,
While mimicking the antiquities of Greek and Roman style

Remembering last fall and our maiden voyage tour, through
The five-pavilion complex in search of artistic lore
Traversing upper-level linkages beneath covered walkways,
Admiring French paneled rooms
Heralding seventeenth-century days

Recalling us seated in the courtyard near cascading
Fountains, scattered with reddish-brown leaves from
Towering trees, each fountain adorned at the base by
Planter-formed showers, filled with contrasting
Arrangements of impatiens flowers

Remembering how we explored the gallery showcase of
European sculptures and master drawings,
Of images from the era of daguerreotypes,
And tempera and gold-on-vellum illuminated manuscripts

Recalling the day I heard an FM radio shout-out from a
Home girl, and followed up with an inquiry that would
Rock our world, the question influenced by the intro to
Patti Labelle's, "When You Talk about Love,"
"this is a test, Shoobie, shoobie, boom, boom, tell me,
what do you know about love?
It's just a test! It ain't yo' life! Tell me."

Remembering how you first denied, but later would confide,
To playing, while at the same time scoring, a breathtaking,
Yet eventually heartbreaking, coed Hoochie Miss,
Whom you claimed lured you to her crib, with a steamy kiss,
And "an offer you couldn't refuse," promise of untold bliss

Recalling how we futilely tried to find a way to make up,
After a six-month lover's quarrel breakup,
And my tearful unraveling when Patti's depth-probing
Peruse, eventually proved, to be so painfully true
"I'd like to give you a test, so darlin' prepare yourself,
When you say love please explain,
What pictures pop in your brain,"

Nobody's Supposed to Be Here

Friday afternoon, New Years Eve '99, and tonight I had an
RSVP to wine and dine, at a Lake Tahoe after-five
"Ovation to the New Millennium," celebration, so
I boarded an LAX flight into Reno's Cannon International,
A crowing finale to an extended winter vacation

Each turn in the winding Nevada road during the hour
Shuttle to the Four Seasons resort, unveiled spellbinding
Images of a picturesque wonderland, which boasted of
Unparalleled winter sport, in route to the tranquility of the
Granlibakken, a mountainous hideaway's wintry break,
That prides itself in living up to
"A hill sheltered by trees," its Norwegian namesake

A traditional host to both alpine and cross-country skiing,
A secluded community of redwood-framed townhomes,
Nestled in a seventy four-acre snow-covered valley,
And surrounded by dense thickets
Of pristine pine forest zones

Its north-shore location just a stone's throw,
From an icy, yet spectacular Lake Tahoe,
With downhill skiing and snowboarding, only minutes away,
As Ski Homewood, Squaw Valley, and Alpine Meadows,
Beaconed enthusiastic weekend warriors to play

An abode, which boasts of cross-country trailheads,
Ice-skating, snowmobiling, sledding, and commuting by
Snowshoe, looking forward to an après-ski warming up and
Winding down rendezvous, eagerly anticipating the quaint
Sauna and spa village hospitality—and you,
A delightful ember to spark a continuation
Of our May-December affair to remember

I closed my eyes and envisioned your smooth ebony
Complexion, felt your tender lips of affection,
Recalled the tight cling of your arms about my waist,
And your firm embrace

Remembered the suspense-filled drama, woven throughout
Your "still waters run deep" screenplay-writing karma,
The slight touch of gray in your closely cut hair,
And your infectious smile, that seemed to beacon me there,
Your five-eleven slender frame,
And wanderlust longing for an exotic travel refrain

Smiling as I reflected on my upbeat tempo, each time I was
With you, it was as though every day signaled, an adventure
Starting anew, and how silly I was to keep slippin' on
Different outfits, in futile attempts to impress,
Because every garment I adorned,
When I was with you, felt like a party dress

And as the van pulled into the resort's semicircular drive,
And gradually rolled to a stop, I momentarily concluded my
Reflections on this ironic paradox, a dilemma, which
Seemed best expressed in lyrics rendered by
Deborah Cox, an R & B songstress,

"So I placed my heart under lock an' key,
Said I'd take some time to take care of me,
How did you get here, nobody's supposed to be here,
I've played that game for the very last time,"

SPEND MY LIFE WITH YOU

Spend My Life with You

You said it was the sweet and sexy sound of my voice,
The way I crossed my right leg over my left, and slowly
Kicked when seated, perhaps by habit, perhaps by choice,
That the power of our love made you quiver from head to
Toe, and caused ripples of passion to flow to the very depths
Of your soul, once again rendering you whole

You said it was the Herbal Essence-scented fragrance in my
Hair, the disgusted look I gave when you whispered
Something silly in my ear, that it was because a light seemed
To flow from my eyes, deep from an inner zone, and it was
Warm and inviting, and beaconed you home

You said that whenever you were near me, your throat
Tightened, your breath quickened, and your heart beat
A million miles a second, and in the goosebump-inducing
Chill of a cool wintry night, your sole desire, was to wrap
Your warmth around me, like a spectacular seashore bonfire

You said that kissing me, reminded you of the sensation of
Savoring, a luscious apple that was juicy and sweet,
That the charismatic aura of my presence, made your world
Feel more complete, and that you were like a
Sparkling blue stream, and I was like a wild white orchid,
Clinging gingerly to your gently sloping, rocky scheme

Recalling last December and my twenty-ninth birthday
Surprise, at Il Cielo's in Beverly Hills on Burton Way,
We had just finished a candlelit Italian entree,
When suddenly a waiter approached, then smiling, handed
Me a bouquet of a dozen long-stem red roses,
Interspersed with white baby's breath sprays

Remembering how you reached into the pocket of your
Sweater vest, retrieved a small black box,
And then held it in the palm of your outstretched left,
As though it were a velvet-covered treasure chest

Recalling how with your right, you gently cradled my hand,
And then whispered in a voice so soft that only I could
Understand, "The sooner the better, don't you think? our
Love is so beautiful, no matter how many years apart in age,
We always manage to respond to each other's
Heart-to-heart page

"Our love is stronger and more determined than life's
Unpredictable sorrows, I surrender my foolish pride,
Because I want you to be a part of my tomorrows,
I get down on my knees every morning and night,
And thank God for creating you, and more than anything
Else, I appreciate the sheer magic
Of every little thing that you do"

And then opening the case to reveal, a brilliant three-stone
Diamond-with-sapphires engagement ring you said, "If I
Could, I would turn back the hourglass of time to make you
Mine," remembering how the tears of joy began to trickle
Down my face, recalling how you tried to dab each moist
Droplet away, with tender touches of handkerchief lace

And remembering you saying, "Now as one Millennium
Draws to an end, the dawning of a new one understood,
I promise to relinquish my confirmed bachelorhood, and, as
Your soulmate, vow to devote the rest of my life, if you
Would grant me the privilege of being my wife."

In the Mood

Cruising the white sandy stretches of Asilomar State
Beach, located on the ocean's edge of the Monterey
Peninsula, in Pacific Grove, California, traversing along
This "Refuge by the Sea," which overlooks an
Ever-surging Pacific Ocean,
Where 105 secluded acres of forests
And dunes seem to be joined in blissful devotion,
En route to Carmel and a sauna adorned with rose
Petals and scented love potion

Recalling how, during rehearsal for our June ceremony,
My bridesmaids half-heartedly promised a teasing
Photographer, that they wouldn't smear their mascara and
Makeup, however, the Kleenex seemed to flow freely
When the vocalist's soulful rendition of, "Suddenly,"
Persuaded their emotions to break up,
A sweetly sentimental and romantic hymn, and
Classic 1984 release by the Whispers and Phyllis Hyman

In many ways the tune painted a colorful portrait of my
Life with the words, "suddenly though it seems,
You're everything to me, the way I always knew,
That lovin' you would be, ooh, and suddenly I am not
Afraid to give love as you gave, for you've become
The light that leads the way,"

Smiling as I recalled your tenderly haunting delivery of
The vows, and my breathy, low-pitched, reply,
"You were the promise of a vision I had yet to see,
It was as though you've always been there for me,
You were the rustle of the leaves
As I walked down the streets,
The smell of softener in my freshly laundered sheets,

You were the cool towel on my brow when I was ill,
The wellspring of my joys, and the
Hearth that warmed me during a wintry chill,
You were like the distant lighthouse
Beacon that guided my way,
And helped me weather life's occasional
Teardrop swells, till I was safely moored at bay,

You were my best friend, and bestowed the kiss,
That awakened me gently,
From the restless slumber of heartache's painful abyss,
And nothing on earth will ever come between us,
As we traverse the race between distance, time, and space"

According to my mother, tradition invites us to adhere
To the principles of, "something old, something new,
Something borrowed, something blue,"
And she honored that custom by pinning
My grandmother's diamond brooch on my gown,

However, perhaps in fun, or perhaps simply
Not to be outdone, my father slipped
My husband a copy of his favorite 1987 vintage Whispers
CD titled, "Just Gets Better with Time," just as we were
Preparing to depart from the wedding-reception line

Smiling, my husband inserted the disc into the CD hood,
And then surprised me by singing along with the lyrics to
The Whispers's sensual rendition of, "In the Mood,"

"Feel much like romancing
How'd you like to wine and dine
I'd like to take you dancin'
Candlelights and dinner (We'll both relax)."

About the Author

Gene Hewett earned a Ph.D. Degree from the University of Southern California Sol Price School of Public Policy, a Master's in Health Administration from the University of California at Los Angeles School of Public Health, and a Bachelor's Degree in Psychology from Claremont McKenna College. He first began teaching on a part- time basis in 1988. Over the years he has served as a lecturer at the University of Southern California, California State University of Dominguez Hills, National University, and the University of Phoenix (UOP). Courses taught were in the areas of research methods, statistics, health behavior, management theory, organizational communication, and grant proposal writing. In addition, at National University he taught a course titled, "Introduction to Literature." Also, at UOP he taught a course titled, "Written Communication." For the past 25-plus years, he has served as an associate faculty member at the University of Phoenix, where he is qualified to facilitate 25 undergraduate and postgraduate courses in the online and classroom modalities.

As President of G.H. Consultants, Inc. his primary duties include the publishing, marketing and promotion of "The Transition, A Novel of Promise, Pitfalls, Perseverance and Passion" and "Wine Me, Dine Me, Dance Me, Romance Me." G.H. Consultants, Inc. is also available to conduct the following secondary activities; (1) grant proposal writing, (2) program evaluations, (3) community opinion surveys, (4) public administration-related policy analyses, (5) legislative analyses, and (6) designing law enforcement training programs.

His earliest publication dates back to 1967, when a short story titled, "Soul Set #5" was printed in the *Claremont Collegian*. The *Collegian*, now titled the *Collage*, is the local newspaper for the Claremont Colleges. Selections from some of the authors' earliest poems were also published in the *Collegian* in 1968 and 1969. These poems were titled "Notes From An Angry Blackman," "Who Am I?" and "Dark Shades." The author cites three courses taken during the Claremont College years as being instrumental to the development of his writing skills. These courses included: fiction writing, an independent study in creative writing, and a senior thesis. The author's senior thesis, titled *A Room Facing the Sunset*, consists of sixty-four pages of poetry, short stories, and an essay. The current collection, titled *Wine Me, Dine Me, Dance Me, Romance Me*, begins with six of these thesis-related poems.

In 1971, during the UCLA period, "Who Am I" was also published in a journal titled *Plexus*. This journal was an annual publication produced by the University of California at Los Angeles Center for Health Sciences. After completion of his Master's in Health Administration in 1972, the author joined the Watts Writers Workshop. He wrote three additional poems contained in *Wine Me, Dine Me, Dance Me, Romance Me* during his one-year stay with the workshop.

The remaining twenty-eight poems were written during the period 1973 to 2000. To date, five of the thirty-seven poems in the collection have been published in various National Library of Poetry anthologies. These include "Ebony Lady" in *Nightfall of Diamonds* (1995), "Firefly" in *A Muse to Follow* (1996), "The Last Time I Saw Spring" in *Best Poems of 1997*, "It's Gonna Take A Miracle" in *Outstanding Poets of 1998*, and "Ain't No Way" in *From the Mountaintop* (2000). In addition, "My Funny Valentine" was published in the Spring/Summer 1997 issue of *Night Roses*.

Appendix

"Conclusion (Dancin')"

"What I'd Say" by Ray Charles

"Crystal Blue Persuasion" by Tommy James and the Shondells

"My Guy" by Mary Wells

"The One Who Really Loves You" by Mary Wells

"My Cherie Amour" by Stevie Wonder

"Superstition" by Stevie Wonder

"Heat Wave" by Martha and the Vandellas

"My Baby Loves Me" by Martha and the Vandellas

"Shotgun" by Jr. Walker and the All-Stars

"Function at the Junction" by Shortie Long

"Soul Man" by Sam and Dave

"Hold On! I'm Comin'" by Sam and Dave

"Reach Out I'll Be There" by The Four Tops

"Still Water (Love)" by the Four Tops

"Thank You" by Sly and the Family Stone

"I'm Your Puppet" by James and Bobby Purify

"Respect" by Aretha Franklin

"Chain of Fools" by Aretha Franklin

"My Girl" by The Temptations

"Ain't Too Proud to Beg" by The Temptations

"Slippin' into Darkness" by War

"It's Your Thing" by the Isley Brothers

"Rock with You" by Michael Jackson

"Don't Stop 'til You Get Enough" by Michael Jackson

"What's Goin' On" by Marvin Gaye

"I Heard It through the Grapevine" by Marvin Gaye

"Rock Steady" by The Whispers

"Love Come Down" by Evelyn "Champagne" King

"Never Knew Love Like This Before" by Stephanie Mills

"Heaven Must Be Missing an Angel" by Tavares

"Paradise" by Sade

"1999" by Prince

"Can't Get Enough of Your Love, Babe" by Barry White

"What's Love Got to Do with It" by Tina Turner

"That's The Way Love Goes" by Janet Jackson

"Love and Happiness" by Al Green

"Another Sad Love Song" by Toni Braxton

"All Day Music" by War

"Early in the Morning" by The Gap Band

"Burn Rubber On Me" by The Gap Band

"Everybody Everybody" by Black Box

"Funkin' for Jamaica" by Tom Browne

"Luv Me, Luv Me" by Shaggy, Janet Jackson

"Last Dance" by Donna Summer

"Conclusion (Romancin')"

"Please, Please, Please" by James Brown

"It's A Man's, Man's, Man's World" by James Brown

"At Last" by Etta James

"I Wanna Know Your Name" by The Whispers

"I Wanna Know Your Name" by The Intruders

"Am I Dreaming" by Atlantic Starr

"Ooh Baby, Baby" by Smokey Robinson and The Miracles

"Let's Fall in Love" by Peaches and Herb

"You Are My Lady" by Freddie Jackson

"Baby I'm For Real" by The Originals

"La-La Means I Love You" by The Delfonics

"Didn't I (Blow Your Mind This Time)" by The Delfonics

"Me and Mrs. Jones" by Billy Paul

"You Are Everything" by The Stylistics

"I'm Not in Love" by Dee Dee Sharp

"Hey There Lonely Girl" by Eddie Holman

"Let Me Make Love to You" by The O'Jays

"Distant Lover" by Marvin Gaye

"Love Ballad" by Jeffrey Osborne

"Fire and Desire" by Rick James and Teena Marie

"I'm So into You" by Peabo Bryson

"Turn Off the Lights" by Teddy Pendergrass

"Come Go with Me" by Teddy Pendergrass

"If You Don't Know Me by Now" by Harold Melvin and the
    Blue Notes

"Hope That We Can Be Together Soon" by Harold Melvin and the
    Blue Notes

"Is It Still Good to Ya" by Nickolas Ashford and Valerie Simpson

"When Will I See You Again" by The Three Degrees